THE BLACK PRINCESS & OTHER STORIES

THE BLACK PRINCESS &
OTHER STORIES

MICHAEL CAMENZULI CHETCUTI

Dedication

Go Baithurumi mmaagwe Letsile

CONTENTS

1

THE BLACK PRINCESS

THE TUTORIAL

She appeared to be of average height when sat in the classroom. It was when she stood up that one could see she was unusually tall, with long thin arms, which hung gracefully by her sides. Her body was quite short in proportion to the rest of her, which gave one the impression of refinement when she moved. She hardly ever spoke, always arriving at the classes early and alone, would invariably seem to be the last to leave the lecture room, which on one particular occasion gave me the opportunity to engage in conversation with her.

She had arrived at the university a couple of weeks into the semester, having missed some classes. There had been an air of mystery as to where she had travelled from, but this quickly disappeared soon after her arrival. 'How are you settling in with the university? I asked. She looked up, from putting her folder in her shoulder bag and as if noticing me for the first time, quite spontaneously broke out into a broad smile that lit up her face, said. 'I am just fine, I'm Ok,' she seemed to correct herself. 'Well, should you need anything, you must let me know, or let us know, we want to make sure that you are getting along alright, whilst you are studying here,' I replied. 'Yes, yes I will, but I am just fine now,' she said. A colleague had entered the classroom, distracting me from the conversation. She had turned and within a moment was through the doorway into the corridor.

The following Thursday afternoon was set aside for tutorials, and when checking my door, I noticed her name in the last two slots of the period. I thought of the conversation we had in the class she had attended at the beginning of the week and wondered why she felt it necessary to want the extended time for a tutorial. She was stood with her arms folded around several files, across from the adjoining corridor, when I ushered the last student through my door. I waited for a moment thinking she would notice, but she appeared to be deep in thought. I called her name, which startled her into life, quickly making her way to my door, saying 'Sorry, sorry.' I waived her to the chair, whilst I stood with my back to the window. She shuffled the files on her lap, before opening one with my module title written across it. She looked up at me, and biting her bottom lip pensively. She appeared reticent to commence talking. I tried to put her at ease by asking her, 'How are you coping with the course material? She shifted herself in an attempt to sit more upright and said, 'The material is just fine, but I have difficulty in accepting some of your cultural approaches to the subject, or more importantly, the aspects and attudes.' I felt a certain indignation in her voice and sensed a note of conflict or argument in her manner. 'But surely you are here to study and describe the cultural aspects of English literature and culture rather than find critism of it,' I said defensively. She seemed to involuntary wince from my remark and I felt a certain justification in my reply, which quickly subsided, when she replied. 'I do not feel it is criticising, when I was simply giving an opinion of a culture so different from my own,' she said quietly. 'But isn't that the reason for your studies here, in order to learn the diversity of other cultures? I asked, trying to match her quiet manner. 'Yes, she nodded, but it is as if your literature reflects all that is outside of a person, rather than that which is inside,' she said politely. I could feel that the conversation was going nowhere, and suggested, 'Why don't you write a short essay about some aspects of your own culture, which may help us to a better understanding of our African students,' I said, trying to be off hand. Her face broke out into a broad smile, and said, 'Okayyy,' drawing out the word as if it were a challenge. 'I should like that very much, but it would be simpler for me to tell it as a story, or in the way of a fable or praise poetry,' she said happily. 'That will be just fine,' I said, and then fell silent hoping she would not think I was mimicking her. In a moment she was stood up, made the slightest bow forward, and was through the door into the corridor.

THE STORY

It was some weeks later into the semester, when I was collecting some of the examined work from my students that I noticed an essay folder with her fine handwriting on it. She had missed several classes and I had been informed by her house-mate that she had been ill, and had handed in the assignment for her. I gave it no importance, but felt an urge to look at her work. On returning to my study, I dropped the heavy files of essays onto my desk, and opening her file, written across in bold letters was, The Black Princess (a true story) I looked at my office clock and noticing that I had a half an hour before my next lecture, I settled into my desk chair and began to read.

There was a time, many many years ago, a small country, which had a king and queen, who had only one daughter. The queen had a difficult time at the birth of the child, which prevented her from having any more children. The king was greatly saddened by this news and devoted his time in trying to rule his kingdom in a fair and just manner. There was everything in the palace the child could wish to have. They would have wonderful parties to celebrate the daughter's birthdays and would dress her in fine silks and present her with precious gifts. The king was a wise man and knowing that his daughter would be his sole heir to the throne, would one day rule over his kingdom, feared that too much material possessions may create a greedy, self-gratifying queen, who would rule his kingdom unwisely. After much consultation with his advisors he decided to send his daughter to a remote village far away. She would there spend many years as an adopted child of a poor childless couple, in order that she may learn and appreciate the eternal values of life.

The secret of the black princess was kept from the childless couple, but were so happy to have been gifted a daughter who could help them, did not concern themselves about her origins. The black princess, being so young, quickly adapted to her new life-style, drawing water from the well and helping her mother with the daily tasks of milking the goats, feeding the chickens, and taking the mid-day meal to her father in the field. Although life was hard for the black princess it was a time of plenty and much happiness was shared between the child and parents. They taught her all the skills and customs of rural life, which she accepted gratefully. The time passed slowly, the rainy seasons bringing rich abundant crops, which in turn provided the couple and daughter with the simple, but enduring pleasures of life. The black princess grew into a tall young girl, shy and unassuming, with a profound respect for her parents and village life.

One day, late in the afternoon a group of strangers entered the village with several animals trailing them. Their manner and clothes were that of people who had travelled far. After the customary greetings from the Kgosi, they enquired of a certain family within the village. They were shown to a small clearing, where a group of huts sat close together, amidst a tiny fenced-off enclosure. Stood near the entrance to one of the huts was a tall young girl, who on seeing the strangers quickly disappeared into the hut. The strangers stopped and waited. Presently, a man and woman came out of the hut carrying small stools, which they placed near the shaded part of the clearing. On seeing this, the strangers called a formal greeting to the couple, which they returned in a polite, but distant manner. The strangers then advanced towards the couple, who in turn offered them to sit.

Nothing was said until the tall young girl reappeared from the hut carrying a jug and small bowls, which having placed them near the group retired into the hut. It was one of the oldest of the group of strangers who spoke first. He commenced to reveal the true identity of the black princess and the reasons for their visit, which was to return her to her rightful place as daughter to their king and queen and future ruler of their land.

The man and woman listened with astonished disbelief and presently sent for their daughter, who after being told the news expressed a wish to stay with the only real parents she knew. The elder member of the group first looked to his fellow travellers, and then speaking directly to her, said, 'With all respect to you my princess, my king and queen, your parents, have given me strict instructions to return you to the palace and your rightful place in our kingdom.' On hearing the insistence in the voice of the elder, she lowered her head, and respectfully desired to be excused. The elder traveller seeing this as an opportunity to speak to the couple alone, nodded assent, wherein the black princess arose and made a token bow to the travellers, walked haltingly, towards the far side of the clearing, squatting near the cooking enclosure.

The conversation which ensued between the travellers and the couple are of little matter here, but suffice to say when they had finished, the man called his daughter to his side, and seeing the sad look on her face, beckoned her to sit. The man waited a moment, composing himself as one might, who was about to give sad news to a dear one. When he had finished the young girl was trembling with emotion her eyes welling over in tears, made a respectful bow to him saying, 'But you are the only real father I have ever known,' correcting herself added, 'The only parents I can ever love, please father do not let them take me to a place where I cannot ever be myself, my place is here with you and mother.' The man gave a brave and gentle smile, saying to the black princess, 'There are many things I have not understood in my life my daughter and this is just one more.' He paused and then said, 'But there is one thing I am certain and that is, you shall never be far away from your mother and me, you will always be here with us in our hearts.' He then turned to the travellers, making a gesture of assent to them, stood, and walked towards his wife waiting near the hut. The black princess, not wishing to disobey her parents returned to her hut.

Within a few moments she reappeared with a small weaved bag, a small jug and bowl hanging from the shoulder strap. The travellers on seeing the black princess walked quickly towards her and making grand gestures, bowed low to her. The elder of the travellers approached her tentatively, placing a purple and gold-lined cloak over her shoulders, whilst ushering her towards one of the animals. She swiftly mounted one and the elder of the group, lead the animal out of the enclosure, respectfully followed by the entourage. Within a few moments they were out of the clearing, heading towards the outskirts of the village.

The black princess on her return to the kingdom was greeted with great pomp and celebration. The subjects stood each side of the entrance to the palace shouting and waving to announce the return of their princess. They threw scented petals of exotic flowers at her feet, whilst bowing low to show their respect. Musicians plucked at their instruments singing songs of praise to her in sweet, dulcet tones. The king and queen gave a public holiday to all their subjects, in order to mark the day of her return. The black princess being young and impressionable took to her new life with a certain bemused astonishment. She saw little of the king and queen except to perform some ceremony or attend some state occasion.

She was often left alone for long periods with her attendants, who treated her in a cool manner in fear of offending her, which may have caused some rebuke from the palace. They marvelled at her simple approach to things, her daily habits, and the way in which she treated each of them with the same politeness and respect, normally saved for the nobility. Unknowingly, she created an atmosphere of tolerance and humility, which appeared out of place in the position she held within the palace. It was not long before she began to pine for her life in the remote village. Especially, the only true parents she had ever known, and the simple things, which she had taken for granted in her old life.

Gradually, she became sickened by her new lifestyle and begged to be taken back to the remote village. On hearing this, the king became frantic, concerned only that he would lose his only heir to the throne, he rushed around to each of his advisors, imploring them to provide a solution, in order to maintain his blood line to the throne. After a long consultation with his advisors, they finally suggested that she should be sent far away to another country where she may study and improve her life experience, other than the village life she had known. The king reluctantly agreed, making one proviso, which was ... '

The story appeared to end in mid-sentence. I suddenly looked up at my study clock, and realising I would be late for my next lecture, decided to wait until her next class, which would be the following Monday morning. I spent most of the following weekend marking students examined work, but could not get the idea of the young African student's story out of my head and in some way began to understand the complex nature of her culture, and the simple way in which she expressed her feelings. I arrived at the class early on Monday morning, in the hope of speaking to her before the class commenced. Her housemate was already there and I sensed a note of trepidation, in her voice when she approached me, saying that the student had received a telephone call on Saturday morning insisting that she return home at once. It appeared that a member of her family was seriously ill. I checked with the house staff, who said, it was the most extraordinary situation. A group of people dressed in traditional African costume had arrived early on Sunday morning, asking after her. They were taken to her room, where they proceeded to make a great fuss over her, helping her to pack, while seemingly whispering to her in a polite and respectful manner. She appeared embarrassed by their presence, and tried to appear off-hand, laughing in a nervous way. She was quickly ushered through the Halls into a large black car. The driver asked us the quickest way to the airport and took off at a frightful speed. The same air of mystery surrounded her departure as did her arrival.

THE LETTER

It was some months later that I received the letter. It had a certain feel about it. The envelope was of a parchment like paper with embossed lettering across the top. There was no stamp, which gave one the impression it was from some embassy. I instinctively knew it may be from the African student, who had left in such a hurry some months earlier. To my surprise it was written in ink and in large letters by someone, who apparently was not in the habit of writing. It was from her father, who commenced by thanking me for all the help I had provided for his daughter, whilst she had studied at our university. It was unfortunate that she could not continue her studies; because she especially enjoyed the tasks I gave her, which helped her to a better understanding of herself and her culture. He then proceeded to explain the reason for her quick departure and flight home. His wife, the queen had suddenly been taken ill, and fearing her demise had requested his daughter to return. Because she would be the sole heir to the throne it was imperative that she take her place by her fathers' side. Fortunately, the queen had made a remarkable recovery on the return of the princess and was now convalescing. The reason for this communication was that the princess had disappeared and was thought to be living in a remote area of his kingdom. He had hoped for a more understanding daughter, but felt it was only a question of time, before she would return to her proper place in the palace. The king had hoped that because of his daughter's affection for her teacher, she might try to contact him. Would he therefore, kindly notify them of any communication he may have with her.

I have often wondered how she must be, far away in that remote village, but that letter was written to me over three years ago and since then I have not heard any news of the black princess.

2

THE PASSING OF PADDY McMAHON

THE WAKE

The parlour was dimly lit and a big open fire was blazing in the grate, lighting up the faces of the group of mourners. Rows of chairs aligned the walls, where they sat quietly, looking at each other, occasionally smiling and nodding to one another in silent recognition.

The parlour door slowly opened and the deceased's sister Noreen, gently stepped in to the room. She lifted the back of a chair and carried it close to the fire and sitting down, rubbing her hands she uttered, 'Be Jesus, Paddy, you certainly picked a cold time to have to peg out on us! Turning to the priest who sat opposite her she said, 'Oh! I am sorry Father Michael that was a bit out of place wasn't it? The priest raised his whiskey glass and taking a large swallow, said, 'Not at all my dear, we are here to celebrate Paddy's passing as well as mourn it and what you said is not at all out of place.'

This seemed to lighten the atmosphere and several mourners started chatting to each other. The priest drained his glass and turning to a huge man sitting next to him asked, 'Shamus, I believe you have brought us a bottle of Pochine with you from the Emerald isle to send our dear Paddy, your brother, to his heavenly home? Shamus, smiled and took a deep breath and sighed, 'Ai! that I have Father Michael and a bloody good sending off is what he is going to get, to be sure.' The mourners chorused, 'Hear! hear! Shamus, best bloody speech you've made in a long time.' Shamus raised his glass and said, loudly, 'Here's to Paddy McMahon, the finest sailor that ever sailed the seven seas.' Everyone, raised their glasses and repeated, 'To Paddy McMahon!

Just then the parlour door opened and a plump, red faced middle aged woman stepped down into the room followed by a West Indian sailor saying, 'Good grief, what on earth is all the commotion about? 'My dear poor Paddy is lying alone there in the front room, laid out to rest and there's a shindig going on in the parlour! Shamus quickly answered, 'Now, now there, Mildred, tis only a little a celebration we be having to honour the passing of our dear brother, it has been most upsetting time for all of us here and quite a shock, especially for dear sister Noreen, who hadn't seen him these past six years.'

She turned to the West Indian and said, 'It must be most upsetting for you too Sidney, to have to leave your ship at Southampton and get here just in time for the funeral.' 'Well, what more could an old shipmate do for his pal, he treated me like a son he did, why I can remember the first time we shipped out together, I was just a lad, fresh from Trinidad and your Paddy took me under his wing.' 'Well, never the less, I do believe in a bit of reverence at a time like this.' she said, quickly putting a handkerchief to her mouth. 'There! There! Mrs McMahon, try not to upset yourself, it's like it has been said, it's been an upsetting time for all of us, Paddy suddenly dying the way he did.' She nodded her head and slowly walked towards the corner table where bottles of wines and spirits and large bottles of stout were neatly stacked next to a row of tall glasses. She poured herself a large Port and quietly sat in a tall-backed chair in the corner. 'What time is the Hearst arriving to collect Paddy in the morning? asked Father Michael, breaking the awkward silence. 'That will be nine o'clock,' answered Noreen. 'Well I best be off, I have a busy day ahead of me tomorrow,' replied Father Michael. 'I was just about to open that bottle of the hard stuff,' said Shamus, reaching down to his small suitcase by his chair. 'Well, in that case, maybe, I should just stay for a wee dram as a nightcap,' said Father Michael.

When the priest finally left the Wake the daylight was just appearing through the slits in the heavy curtains, Shamus was passed out across his chair snoring loudly.

ST. JOHN THE BAPTIST CHURCH

The coffin was laid at the foot of the altar, with a large Irish flag, draped across the corner. A large photograph of Paddy was stood in front of it. It was an earlier photograph of him, showing him wearing his Matelot top and a white sailor's hat, tilted on the side of his head. At the front row to the left of the aisle sat Mildred, followed by Sidney, Noreen and Shamus. Music softly played in the background and a gentle Irish tenor voice was singing, 'If you ever go across the sea to Ireland … 'Father Michael suddenly appeared, unsteadily from behind a purple curtain, as the last refrain, '… and watch the sun go down on

Galway bay.' The congregation stood up to acknowledge the presence of the priest. The priest placed a black file book on the pulpit and clearing his throat, said solemnly, 'Today we celebrate the life of' and looking down at his black book, said, 'Patrick Hennessey McMahon.'

There was a sudden sound of someone weeping in the front aisle and a lady in the second aisle passed a handkerchief to Noreen, who reached over and passed it to Mildred. Father Michael, gave Mildred a beatific smile and continued, 'Paddy McMahon, as I knew him was a lovely kind and generous man and I am still puzzled as to why the good Lord decided to take him from us, when he was due to retire from the sea in only a few short months.'

He raised his hands in disbelief and added, 'Of course there are people here today who new Paddy far better than I and I shall in due course call on them to join with us and celebrate his life and times.' Sidney, was the first to rise and clutching a large brown envelope in his hand, he mounted the Rostrum and drawing out a two page letter from the envelope, placing his glasses on his head, he said, 'I can't say enough of what a good man Paddy had been to me, indeed both Mrs McMahon and Paddy have been like a Mother and Father to me,' he added. Mrs McMahon, continued to sniffle, eyes lowered, nodding her head in agreement. He continued with a year by year account of his life and times at sea and at home with his best pal Paddy. He added, 'Mrs McMahon has been much too upset to speak today and she has asked me to read a poem she has written about her life with Paddy.'

The poem gushed sentiment and after each stanza, she would end with, '... and that was my Paddy! Several other guests stood up and spoke in the same vein, Shamus having drifted off into a stupor, during Sidney's speech.

They managed to shake Shamus awake when it came to lift the heavy coffin and a pallbearer at each corner carried the casket down the long aisle of the Saint John the Baptist's Church. At the entrance to the church, the Ushers took over from the pallbearers and slid the casket into the Hearst. Other Ushers followed with large wreaths and draped them each side of the casket. The largest read, To Paddy, my darling husband. The Principal Usher dressed in black, with a long black coat and black top-hat, slowly walked in front of the Hearst, holding a long black stick in his right hand. The hard winter frost dusted the pavements with white powder and frozen snow slush filled the gutters. The cortège followed in several black cars, slowly passing the Pilotage Office, which looked out onto the bay, finally turning left at the Westgate, over the railway sidings, before heading out towards the cemetery.

TO THE CEMETERY

The trip to the cemetery was slow and several men on pavements lifted their trilbies as a mark of respect for the passing funeral procession. People waiting at bus stops, huddled in shop doorways to avoid the cold biting wind of the February morning. Inside the first car, Mildred, head lowered, held a large white handkerchief to her face, sobbing quietly. Shamus sat next to Sidney, eyes closed, head swaying from side to side with the movement of the car. Noreen sat opposite staring out at the slow moving traffic.

The large black wrought iron gates of the cemetery were forced open against large drifts of snow and rock salt was scattered at the entrance. The Hearst approached the gates making a wide berth to avoid the frozen snow, but started to slide to the left of the gates on the hard frozen ice. The Hearst stopped and after a few minutes the driver climbed out and began to survey the best way to negotiate the gates. Sidney and Shamus, both big men got out of the first car following the Hearst and after speaking to the driver, decided to push the Hearst from behind. Several other men got out of cars and assisted them. The Hearst slowly started to move and Shamus and Sidney, both shoulder to the left of the Hearst pushed and heaved. The Hearst slowly began to move to the right and crept through the cemetery gates, back wheels spinning on the ice. 'Heave! Shouted Shamus and the Hearst suddenly lurched forward, Shamus sliding down on his hands and knees on the hard ice. 'B'Jesus! cried Shamus, quickly standing up, wiping his wet cold hands on his long black overcoat. He then steadied himself on the cemetery gates and bending, threw up on the frozen snow. 'Blessed Mary and Joseph! he cried, 'That's been sitting on my stomach all morning'. 'Better out then in, eh! Shamus,' said Sidney, grinning. Shamus, wiped his mouth with the sleeve of his black coat and climbed back into the following car.

They arrived at the grave, just as the gravediggers were finishing off. They hurled their shovels over the large earth mound and taking Shamus aside spoke to him. Shamus pushed his hand down deep in his pocket, passed something to the gravedigger, who tipping his hat, waved to his men and walked off the their hut. The Ushers had placed the coffin on the stand, next to the grave, having wrapped the lowering straps across the coffin and now stood a respectable distance away from the family and friends.

Father Michael stood solemnly at the graveside, Mildred and Shamus standing each side of him. Noreen and the rest of the friends and family stood in a half circle around the open grave. A fine sleet slanted across the group and Father Michael, head bowed, opening his missal at its mark, cleared his throat and said solemnly. 'For as much as it has pleased Almighty God to take out of this world the soul of, Patrick Hennessey McMahon we therefore, commit his body to the ground, looking for that blessed hope when the Lord Himself shall descend from heaven with a shout, with the voice of the archangel and with the trump of God and the dead in Christ shall rise first, then we which are alive and remain shall be caught up together with them in the clouds, to meet the Lord in the air and so shall we ever be with the Lord, wherefore comfort ye one another with these words Amen! 'Amen! replied the congregation.

The Ushers stepped forward and with assistance of Shamus, Sidney and two members of the family lifted the casket over the mouth of the grave. They held the straps firm and carefully lowered the coffin down in to the grave, releasing the straps at one end and pulling them up through to the top of the grave.

Father Michael closed his missal and stooping, picked up a clod of earth from the mound and raising his eyes to the heaven's, said, 'May the body and soul of the dearly departed, be laid to rest, ashes to ashes and dust to dust,' tossing the earth in to the grave. The rest of the congregation followed suit, saying their goodbyes. 'God bless you, dear brother, you are now with Mam and Dad,' said Shamus, head bowed. Mildred just stumbled past the grave sobbing loudly as Sidney held her arm to steady her. Noreen just stood over the grave, frozen as the snow and ice surrounding it. She stayed long after the congregation had left and Shamus returning, held her by the arm and gently led her away from the graveside, saying, 'Now come on girl, there is no point in staying, let's get you back to the house, before you catch a chill.'

'He was my big brother! cried Noreen, 'I remember my first day at school, I was frightened being away from Mam for the first time and he comforted me in the playground and walking with me home after school,' she sobbed. 'I feel so guilty not seeing him for those many years and him dying suddenly like that.' 'There! there! said Shamus, 'He's probably better off than most of us and he is with Mam and Dad now,' he added. Noreen nodded her head and turning, allowed Shamus to slowly walk her back to the cars waiting at the Cemetery gate entrance.

FAREWELLS

The fire blazed brightly in the parlour and the chairs were stacked in the corner to make room for a barrel of ale to be propped on a corner stool. Shamus
filled the glasses and passed them round to the menfolk. He tilted each glass
and dropped his hand to create a white foaming head. 'Drink up! me hearties,'
he shouted. 'This is how it all started,' he chuckled. 'Careful, with that bitter
Shamus, there is a special ward at the Mental hospital, for drinkers of that
brew,' said, Father Michael. 'Ai! Don't worry about that none, Father, my brain
is already well and truly pickled,' he replied.

Noreen, was sat in the corner opposite, a half tumbler of whiskey held in her
lap and turning to Mildred, nodding to Shamus said, 'I hope he is going to be
in a fit state to drive me to the train station, I have got to get the ten o'clock
overnight Ferry from Liverpool to Dublin.' 'Don't worry Noreen', Mildred
said, 'I will ask Sidney to share a taxi with you, he's got to be going shortly
anyway.' Mildred turned and shouted to Sidney above the laughter and loud
talk. 'Yes, I can certainly do that Mrs McMahon,' said, Sidney, 'Just give me
five minutes to call a taxi and get my shoulder bag,' 'Thank you Sidney, I'll see
you to the door.'

The taxi hooted its horn and they opened the front door to let him know
they were ready. 'Good night Sidney and safe journey to Southampton,' said
Mildred. 'Good night Mrs McMahon,' said Sidney. They helped Noreen with
her suitcase into the taxi and rolling down her window, she was about to say
something to Mildred but suddenly turned away, rolling the window up. The
taxi drove off in the direction of the Great Western Railway station. Mildred,
slowly closed the front door and passing the front room, looking in, she shuddered with cold and quickly climbed the stairs to her bedroom.

In the parlour the party was in full swing and Shamus was arguing with an
old friend of Paddy's. 'Those gravedigger's are bunch of bloody crooks, if you
ask me,' he said, 'They touched me for a tenner all because they had a job
digging the bloody grave, they said, it had been frozen solid.' Someone in the
party shouted,' Quiet! Gerry from Killarney's going to sing us an Irish song.'
Gerry, stood up, sticking out is chest, began, 'Only a lad of eighteen summers,
but there's no one can deny, when he went to death that morning, proudly held
his head on high.'

'Oh! For Jesus Christ's sake! someone interrupted, 'Can't you brighten it up a bit? 'Hear! Hear! Shouted Shamus, 'How about Paddy McGinty's Goat! And hands on his hips, started raising his knees and twirling around on his toes, raising arms above his head. The party members started clapping a rhythm to each step, shouting, 'Come on Shamus ! He finally twirled himself into the corner where the barrel of ale stood on the stool, tipping it onto the floor. He struggled to pick it up and said, with wet beer soaking his trousers, 'B'Jesus, I hope that's blood.' They all roared with laughter.

The winter night had come down quickly and Father Michael, being much worse for drink, gave his apologies and waved his farewell to the party. 'Good night Father Michael! they chorused. The priest let himself out through the back garden avoiding the main road, slipping through back lanes until he finally arrived at the Presbytery door. God, these Irish funerals, he thought to himself, must get to bed, early mass tomorrow.

The cemetery gates were now locked and Paddy's grave had been filled in and raked over. Far away, over the water Paddy's parents lay, Mary, nee Flanagan and Padraig McMahon. And then there was Paddy McMahon, new to the earth, alone, wrapped in his shroud, waxen faced, oblivious to the waking world.

THE PASSING

And so Patrick Hennessey McMahon had finally been laid to rest. In his passing the house is now quiet. In the front room the coffin trestles lean up against the fireplace and the candles are burned low in their brass holders. In the parlour the fire has burnt out, except for the smouldering smoke, still swirling up the chimney. In the corner propped on a stool an empty barrel of strong ale, its tap open, dripping beer. On the floor, empty bottles of stout are strewn around the seats and the corner table has two half-drunk glasses of whiskey and an empty soda syphon.

The hallway is dark and damp, but if you care to quietly climb the stairs, walk along the landing and pause at Paddy and Mildred's bedroom, you will hear hushed whispers, coming from inside.

'Oh! Sidney I do so honestly miss Paddy, you know, he was so good to me all those years, I can't imagine how I am going to cope without him,' she said, raising her voice. 'Keep your voice down Mildred, for Christ's sake, will you, these walls are thin, do you want someone to hear us? He panted.

THE CYCLIST

THE JOURNEY

He had seemed to have been riding for an age and wished desperately for an opportunity to rest. The others could not be far behind now, he thought to himself, and peered over his shoulder to see in the distance a group of cyclist coming up fast behind him. Fear gripped him and he held the handlebars tighter in an effort to urge the cycle faster along the road. He peddled crouched over the cycle afraid to look up at the long road ahead, sucking air spasmodically between clenched teeth with such effort that made him cry out from time to time in reply to the anguish he felt for his pursuers. How did it ever get this way he thought, how could I have been such a fool to have trusted them, when all the time they were scheming against him, quietly planning to reduce him to this, he thought. But there again, there reasons seemed reasonable considering how they always appeared pleasant and friendly whenever they wanted to get to him. This time though, they had gone too far, and would not let them persuade him with their promises of paradise. He did not want to be saved from eternal damnation; he liked wickedness and being angry, it made him feel different somehow, an individual, someone to be reckoned with, something to be owned.

There was a bend in the road and the cyclist steered his cycle awkwardly into the bushes skirting the road, hidden from his pursuers. He dropped the cycle to the ground and crouched behind a bush, still panting heavily, waiting for them to pass.

They were now coming, almost silently except for the sound of tyres hissing on the tarmac. There must have been at least a hundred of them grouped together, as if in an effort to block the road from the oncoming travellers.

He suddenly felt an uncontrollable urge to let his pursuers see him and stood erect as they passed feeling triumphant that he had outwitted them, laughing white-faced and trembling as they sped passed without noticing him. 'I'm here! he shouted waving his hands above his head. 'I'm here! he screamed, puzzled at their indifference towards him. Soon a realisation came to him and a smile broke over his pale countenance and thought, why are they behaving in this way. He waited until the cyclist's had passed over the horizon and turned to resume his place where he had left the bicycle.

He sat down on the grass, a slight drizzle had started, creating a fine mist, which obscured the road ahead. He all at once felt a calmness wash over him, all fear subsiding with a feeling of utter peace. He wondered how it had become so confusing, trying to recall the events preceding to this last bout of anxiety.

He had awoken early that morning and had envisaged taking a ride into the countryside. It was always so much more pleasant being out riding alone. He always returned home feeling exhilarated by the fresh country air and the physical exercise. This morning proved to be one of those fine days, until his father had purposely started an argument about a trivial matter concerning tardiness. He had tried to avoid the confrontation feeling it would spoil his day, but he always succumbed to his fathers' cruel and sarcastic way of forcing his will upon him.

He had left the house behind a volley of hot words being shouted after him. He remembered his mother, coming down the garden path after him and the look of sympathy, which always made him feel all the more guilty for engaging in useless arguments with his father. She had tried to stop and talk to him, but in his anger, pushed past her, within a moment had mounted his cycle and was safely out onto the open road.

He now felt a twinge of conscience about his behaviour to his mother. She always showed an understanding toward him, often trying to shield him from her husbands' aggressive ways. He made a mental note of making amends to her on his return home and decided that he would set off, as soon as the rain subsided. He now felt a weariness descend upon him and for the first time wondered how he had arrived at this spot in the countryside. It was quite un-familiar to the normal route he took and thought he must have taken a wrong turning some way back. He then remembered the incident with the group of cyclists' and knew something was terribly wrong. He tried to stand, steadying himself, in order to raise the cycle level with his side and trying to mount, felt himself sway, letting go of the cycle, in order to check himself. He seemed to be falling for an age, before landing softly on the wet grass, the fine rain gently playing on his face. He tried to move, but felt as though a heavy weight was holding him down. He peered into the mist and could see vague dark objects looming above him, but feeling surprisingly calm, gave way to all resistance and fear to what was happening. He felt as though he was an observer, as if in the audience in some kind of play.

He was at his first day at school, stood with his back against the playground wall. He was frightened, away from his mother for the first time and felt fear and dread as the older children ran and screamed running around the playground. The cacophony of sound dazed him and he pressed his back close to wall. It was then late the same afternoon, the teacher had told the children to place their hands on their desks and to rest their heads on their hands for a little sleep. He now began to feel calm from the days' turmoil, awoke and was now seven years old, stood with his mother in a cinema queue.

Next, he was in the foyer walking past the pictures of famous film stars, the red plush velvet carpet and dark maroon wallpaper, giving off a feeling of opulence. He had never been happier in his life. The film would transport him to a place far away in the universe, where he would play out his dreams. The picture faded and he was now eleven, sat on the edge of his bed staring out into the garden on a bright summers' day. He felt utter despair, and sadness, deep in thought, puzzled by a feeling of futility. In the distance he could hear the shouts and laughter of children playing in the park near his home. The hall clock chimed four o'clock. Soon he would hear his mothers' gentle footfall on the stairs, the soft tap on the door. 'Dear, are you coming down? It's such a lovely day, you shouldn't lock yourself away on such a nice day.'

The picture faded and changed to where he was sat in the reference library near the memorial plaque, which gave the names of the fallen in the First War. The large skylight windows shone bright beams of sunlight across the library hall, casting dark shadows near the newspaper stands. He could smell the fragrance of fresh wax and turpentine polish given off by the warmth of the sunlight.

He felt at complete peace with himself, and wished the day would never end. The sun moved slowly across the hall, the bright light dazzling his eyes. Unable to read, he placed the book on the table, and closing his eyes, was transported to his last day at school and the feeling of freedom, as if being released from a long period of confinement.

He was leaving the school behind him, turning to take one more look at the green iron railings, which had imprisoned him. He was once more alone riding along a country road, a fine rain soaking his cotton shirt, his face alight with happiness. He was now freewheeling down a steep hill, the wheels racing to the sound of tyre on wet road. He was approaching a crossroads. The picture faded.

ARRIVAL

The day nurse checked off the traces on the instrument panel, near the side of the bed. The room was in darkness, except for the glow of the nightlight, which lit the left side of the cyclists' body. A crepe stretch bandage was wrapped around his head, crossing each side, leaving bare his face. The new relief nurse entered the room softly tiptoeing towards the bed. 'How is he? She whispered. 'Oh, there's no need for quiet with this one, he's well out of it and hasn't regained consciousness from his accident, five months since,' she said loudly. She straightened out the top cover on the bed, tucking in the edges under the mattress. She had supervised the night duty since the arrival of the patient, and completed her duty report by checking off the progress chart hung on the end of the bed. She passed the report to the night nurse, jokingly saying, 'Don't fall asleep, he may wake up, see you about seven.' and was out through door, closing it shut behind her.

The night nurse sat beside the bed, picked up a magazine, flicking through the pages, thinking about the long night ahead. She momentarily glanced at the cyclists face and imagined she had seen a slight flicker of his eyes. Looking across at the traces on the instrument panel, she thought she had seen the end trace of activity fading on the screen.

'No dear, not in front of the boy, please he's only a child! The cyclist was stood in front of his father, head bowed while he was screamed at. His mother was stood between them imploring her husband to stop. The cyclist raised his head while his father continued to rave, the sound reminding him of his first day at school in the playground and the feeling of utter helplessness. But now the noise began to subside until there was silence. He watched bemused as his father ranted and noticed white spittle begin to form on his fathers' angry mouth. The scene faded and a twilight world took its place. He was lying on a large bed where all around him was utter darkness.

The night nurse awoke with a start, the dawn light just breaking through the drawn curtains, casting a beam of light across the cyclists' bed. The bedclothes appeared to have been disturbed, giving the impression of the cyclist lying in a blanket of white driven snow. His face was ashen, softened by the dawning grey light. The nurse startled by the image, jumped up to reach for the wall light switch, bathing the room in a bright white neon light. Feeling more composed she straightened the linen bed cover, before studying the recorded traces on the instrument panel. There had been activity throughout the night, but most of it was sporadic. She made a note on his progress chart and would mention it to the doctor on his morning visit. She yawned, stretched her arms above her head and sat back down in the chair next to the cyclists' bed. She looked at the motionless figure and felt guilty at having fallen asleep while on duty. She checked her watch and noted there was still over two hours before her relief took over, but decided to leave the room lights on, in case of falling asleep again. She looked at the cyclist motionless, except for the slightest breathing, slow and regular. How peaceful he seemed, far away in his comatose world, free of all care and worry.

The cyclist was crouched in the back seat of the classroom, while the nun chalked lines of tables, each ending with an equals sign. She finished writing and turning to the class said, 'Right, who is going to help me with the answers to these sums? The cyclist crouched even lower in his seat terrified at the thought of being picked out to stand up in front of the class. These situations always embarrassed him and made him feel foolish, whenever he was asked. He would invariably guess at the answer, which brought sniggers and restrained laughter from the class. A girl was asked to stand, which brought a feeling of relief to his anxiety. 'You have to divide by six and take away two, which leaves eight,' she said proudly. 'Very good, Mary,' said the teacher, and looking towards the cyclist, pointing to the next line of numbers said, 'And this one? The cyclist froze, and pretending not to have noticed, looked down at his desk. 'It is no use trying to hide behind Tommy Hayes,' the teacher said, as she walked between the desks towards the cyclist. This brought a roar from the class, as they all turned towards the cyclist. The cyclist slowly rose from his seat, his legs shaking. He began to feel faint, and grabbed the edges of his desk to steady himself. The teacher was now stood quite close to him, and flicking the long cane against her heavy skirts said. 'Are you going to keep us waiting all day? The class broke out into peals of laughter and hands shot up to answer the question for her. 'Miss! Miss! they chorused, each delighted at the thought of answering the question. 'No! no! she said, emphatically, pointing the cane at the cyclists' shoulder. 'I want this one to answer the question.' The cyclist straightened up and said, 'You have to mmm.' He was trying to say multiply, but these ordeals always brought on a fit of stammering. A faint smile broke out on the teachers' face, and said, 'What on earth are you mumbling at, speak up boy! The classroom became hazy and the cyclist could feel himself falling towards the nun. She tried to move back, but was too late. She raised her hands to protect herself, but the cyclists' head collided with the nuns' crisp white head-dress, pushing it aside, revealing a skein of long black hair, and lily-white bodice. 'To the headmaster's room! screamed the nun, as she adjusted her blouse and head dress.

The cyclist had been standing outside the headmaster's room, for what seemed ages. He tried to suppress his nervousness and fear, but it kept returning and he began to feel physically sick. The sister had been talking with the headmaster with the door slightly open and the cyclist strained his ear to listen in to the conversation. Suddenly the door swung open and the nun moved swiftly passed the cyclist without raising her head. The headmaster shouted for the cyclist to enter. The headmaster was a giant of a man, and stood with his hands behind his back to the large window in his office. The cyclist, head bowed, stepped quietly into the headmasters' office.

In a moment the headmaster had strode forward grabbing the cyclists' wrist, twisting it palm upwards, and producing a long cane from behind his back, began to raining stroke after stroke on the cyclists' outstretched palm. He then threw away the cyclists' hand and repeated the strokes on his other palm, whilst uttering curses under his breath. The cyclist cried out in pain, and with a mighty effort pushed the headmaster away from himself, and ran out of the office corridor into the main hall. His hands by now had become swollen, and were burning with the sting of the canes' strokes. He felt humiliated, and his eyes filled with tears. He tried to wipe his face with back of his hands, then holding them to his cheeks to stop the burning pain radiating from his palms. He had arrived at the bicycle shed in the playground and rode out onto the main road, trying to grip the middle bar of the chrome handlebars, in order to relieve the pain of his burning palms. He decided not to go home in fear of being reprimanded by his father, but instead set out on the tree-lined road, which led to the countryside.

He finally slowed down to where the lane widened into a area set aside for travellers, who wished to stop for a break in their journey. There were several wooden tables and seats set back off the road, and a large group of cyclists' sat on the grass verge, some stood, leaning their bikes against the tables and seats.

He decided not to stop, but pressed on. He looked back and noticed some of the cyclists' had mounted their frames and were now attempting to follow him. Some stood high on their bikes pushing the frames forward in an effort to catch up with him. They were now waving to him and shouting for him to stop. He raced on in an effort to distance himself, but felt that they were catching up with him. He seemed to be riding for an age and wished desperately for an opportunity to rest.

JOURNEYS END

The doctor looked at the progress chart and then at the cyclist lying prostrate on the bed. The night nurse had just been explaining the irregular trace activities during the night, but the doctor shook his head, put the chart back on the end of the bed, and said, 'I'm afraid we will have no luck with this poor devil, we have just received the last set of scans from the lab, and there is no chance of him ever regaining consciousness.' The day nurse had just entered the room and hearing the end of his conversation, added, 'His parents are outside, should I tell them you would like to speak to them?

The doctor nodded and straightened himself in an effort to compose himself. He could never get used to these interviews and dreaded the usual reaction from the patient's families. There was a gentle tap on the door and the cyclists' parents were shown into the room, the nurse discretely, exiting and closing the door quietly behind her.

The man was quite tall and carried the air of a military officer. His face was firm and showed no trace of anguish. His wife was small and birdlike, with tiny hands that clutched the clasp of her handbag. Her face was delicate, and fine boned, and wore an expression of desolation.

It was her husband, who spoke first saying, 'It's been a terrible ordeal for us, you know, we gave him the finest childhood any young boy could wish for,' he paused, then said, 'We sent him to the best school we could afford' and turning to his wife said. 'Didn't we dear? 'We could never understand his ways, always alone, never wanting to listen to his fathers' advice. We've always been strong in the church, but he could never settle down, I often said, a spell in the army would do him the world of good.' He turned discretely to the doctor and taking him to one side, said, 'You know, I blame a lot of this on his poor mother, always pampering him, never allowing him to grow up, he never had his head out of a book, terrible times we had with him, terrible times.'

4

THE DEATH AND LIFE OF KEFHILWE

EPILOGUE

She never thought or tried to remember when she first started talking to herself. In fact she saw it more a way of communicating with her feelings, but nevertheless, she always listened and spoke with calm attentiveness. It had just finished raining and the warm sun had created a sweet pungent smell of the soil. The seasonal rains had been heavy flooding the lower part of the clearing. Ever since she was a child, she came to this place to sit and think. She spent many a sunset sat with her warrior husband in silence.

Without prompting she heard herself say out loud. 'Yes I am very happy thank you.' and fell silent again. Quite startled to hear herself replying to someone she looked around the clearing to see if anyone could have heard her.

Kefhilwe had always felt in some way outside of things, but had never dared mention it for fear of worrying her husband warrior. Family life had been good, and considering the uncertain times we live she thought, did not wish to invite, nor add any more problems to it. Her husband warrior had been past a long time and knew that it was only a question of time that she would soon join him. Maybe that is what it is, she thought. A kind of wishful waiting to see him again and her odd way of talking in her head when she felt lonely. Most of all she could never hide her loneliness from her husband and always longed to be close with him. Their lives together had been happy and now the warrior cubs had grown, she often thought that time was much too generous with her. 'Kefhilwe! Kefhilwe! said the voice. 'Who is it? she cried. 'Kefhilwe! 'Kefhilwe! the voice said again in a whisper. 'Please, please I am frightened,' pleaded Kefhilwe, to the voice. 'Please tell me what you want? 'Kefhilwe,' the voice said softly, 'I have come to take you home.'

'But I am already home,' she said defensively,' 'Kefhilwe,' said the voice, 'I have spoken with your husband warrior and he is waiting for you,' and added,

'Kefhilwe, listen to me, for a long time I have been preparing a homecoming for you with your husband warrior and all your brothers and sisters, and Kefhilwe you will never feel alone again,'

She was no longer sat in the clearing, but was now suspended high above the trees gazing down in awe at the source of the voice. An unimagined blissful beam of sunlight was streaming through and around her with such intensity that she began to weep with joy and for the first time in her existence she knew that she had never been alone, outside or apart of things and had always belonged.

When the family finally found her she was lying face down in the long grass near the water's edge. They were glad that no predators had scented her whereabouts, and her first born son, Tuelo, head bowed, carried her back to her hut.

CHILDHOOD

Kefhilwe was last born of the children, the parents having long since thrilled to the thought of a new addition to the family. Whilst her older brothers and sisters ran around the clearing, shouting gleefully to each other, she would sit, quietly watching, near her mother's side. Kefhilwe's mother had a difficult birth with her, some saying it was because of the child's frailty. She was altogether a small delicate child, who struggled with the everyday living things, which puzzled her and showed in her shy, unassuming face.

Her parents toiled hard with the dry arid soil of the clearing, eking out a bare living from the father's weaving. Her father was a reserved diffident man, but was respected and admired for his skills as a weaver and the good council he would bring to the family gatherings. It had been whispered around the clearing that his ancestors were from a far distant land and had settled long ago, prospering as local chiefs and griots. But that was a time when the rains were plentiful and would flood the lower part of the clearing, forming small streams, where water could be drawn and the cattle could drink. They now had to walk many hours to draw water from a water-hole, which on occasions would be dry. Her mother appeared to be quite cold and distant at first, and seemed to have inwardly disciplined herself against showing any emotion. But her true character was revealed whenever there was a family member sick or in need of help. It was then that she would be eager to provide words of comfort, staying day and night to nurse the sick member of the family.

This was the time when peoples were united as one family, caring little about traditional families, but viewed anyone who came to the clearing as a family member. Although, Kefhilwe loved her mother, brothers and sisters, she had a special closeness with her father, who always seemed to understand her odd ways. Whenever she was upset he would pick her up, and carry her to his weaving place, sit her down next to him while he worked away at a piece of cloth. She in turn would take on a pensive look as if she understood her father's work, passing him bits of wool, which had been trimmed from the weave. He would play the little game, whispering how helpful his last born was and how one day she would take his place at the weave. Kefhilwe was an unusually gifted child, which showed in her relationship with her family and the clearing. She would intuitively know about matters within the community, without any council from them. This would at first bring peals of laughter from the aunts and uncles, whenever she would utter some remark, which was beyond her years. The time came when the laughter ceased and her comments became a way of interrupted hushed whispers, which invoked embarrassed glances from the elder family members.

During the rainy season the children would squat together, near their parent's huts, daring each other to run out into the great sheets of rain, falling heavily on the red earth. Kefhilwe would run around the clearing, hands held high, beckoning the rain to fall on her, asking the rain how long she would have to wait to grow tall. 'Sister rain, make me grow quickly, because I am tired of being a child, make my breasts grow and give me strong legs, so I may run with the hunt.' Very early on, Kefhilwe withdrew from playing with her siblings, preferring the quiet of her mother's side or the weaving place. She liked the company of the elder members of the family, who in turn saw her as an odd child who may need special care and attention in preparing her for adulthood. The truth may have been was that they forgot how to play as a child, and could never know the unquestioned innocence, which one may only see in the very young.

One day, when her father was laying out the small pieces of fabric ready for stitching together he noticed Kefhilwe looking up into the large fruit tree, near the goat pen, and seemed to be whispering to the tree. He crept softly up behind her. Sensing his presence, she turned, smiled and a few small birds flew away up out of the tree. 'What were you doing, my child? he asked gently. 'I was listening to the birds chatting together and wondered if I may learn their language and talk with them. I tried to say a few words to them, but they took no notice and kept on chattering,' she said, in quite a serious manner. Her father smiled and said. 'What a strange daughter I have talking to birds. Why don't you go and play with your brothers and sisters, instead of such silly games.' Kefhilwe seemed not to have heard her fathers rebuke and said, 'Paba, do you think a bird may want me for a friend and sit with me, while I help you with the weave? 'Yes, I am sure they would,' he said. 'But first you will have to make an effort to play with your brothers and sisters, as well little daughter.' Kefhilwe looked away from her father and said, 'Yes, Paba, I will try, and then we may all play together.' She then looked up into the tree, but seeing the birds had not returned, she made an attempt to respectfully leave her father, stealthily walking towards the cooking hut where several small birds were pecking around the doorway.

There came a time when her mother was preparing the new crop of seeds for sowing and Kefhilwe was given the task of separating them in the large shallow wooden bowls, before sowing. She was very exacting in her tasks and would carefully ensure that no seeds were mixed, nor left on the hut floor. She had once told her mother that if a seedling became mixed up with another type and grew up with them, it may feel a bit out of place with not being with its brothers and sisters.

RITUALS AND STORIES IN THE NIGHT

The ink black night sky was ablaze with bright stars. The communal fire burned brightly, lighting the faces of the children who sat with their uncles and aunties, listening to the stories of times long past. They were told about the five stars that appear at the commencement of ploughing and sowing of new crops and how it was important to wait till they were at the summit of the night sky. How it was told that at a certain time of a season when the sheep would all sit in a line during a certain night, staring eastward till dawn, when they would group together in a circle and sleep throughout the day. It was a special day when people prayed together and exchange gifts and sang special songs to commemorate the day. The main meal was always special when they ate roast chicken and rice, instead of the brown maze with sour cream, which was their usual daily meal.

Kefhilwe had lived fourteen of these seasons and was now being prepared for her adult life. One morning she ran to her mother crying of pains in the abdomen and her mother looking down, took her to the goat pen and tied her to a post, before calling Kefhilwe's paternal aunt, who prepared a foul smelling red clay mixture and covered Kefhilwe from head to foot. They kept Kefhilwe in the goat pen for another twelve sunsets and did not allow a male relation near the pen.

Early next morning her aunt untied her and led her out of the pen into the bright sunlight. She squinted in the light and looking around saw her older brothers stood in a line holding long sapling sticks. They swished them back and forth and advanced towards her. She cried out and stood behind her aunt who moved quickly away. Turning round she saw her mother and father near the weaving hut and called out to them. They turned away and disappeared into the hut.

'No! no! She cried and made a run for the weaving hut, but they were soon on her, swishing the sapling across her back and legs. She fell to the ground and begged them to stop, but they continued relentlessly, till they drew blood.

She must have passed out because when she came too, she was lying on a rush mat in a visitors hut. She had been washed clean of the red clay and was wrapped in a goat's skin. Her body had been anointed with special healing herbs and oils, but her skin still smarted from the whipping she received from her brothers.

Kefhilwe's paternal aunt came to the hut the following evening and sitting on the edge of the cot said to her, 'You are now becoming a young woman, which carries responsibilities and your uncles son has shown an interest in you and wants to claim you for his own.'

'But I am far too young for that and I want to keep my freedom and work with my father at the weave, like it has been promised to me,' replied Kefhilwe. The paternal aunt looked at her and continued, 'It is not for you to decide, but what your uncles and aunties agree' and added, 'Your cousin will make a fine husband for you and give you many offspring's.'

'But it is not natural,' replied Kefhilwe, I want to be the one to decide who I wish to share the rest of my life with,' she added.

The paternal aunt stood up and was about to leave the hut, but turning, said, 'Kefhilwe, your family are most concerned about you and they feel that your union with your cousin will help you settle down to family life.'

'I do not understand you or my family for that matter, there is nothing wrong with me, I just feel different, that is all and prefer my own company,' she replied. The paternal aunt looked at her ruefully and said, 'Do you mean the company of birds, which you are often, caught talking to, or when it rains you chatter away to the clouds?

Kefhilwe replied, 'I see nothing wrong with that, they are creatures and things just like us, they live and breathe just like us, they sing just like us, I do not see them any different to us,' she replied. The paternal aunt could see this was getting her nowhere and shaking her head, said, 'Prepare yourself for your union which will be after two sunsets,' and turning left the hut.

Kefhilwe lay back down on the cot, moving to a position to reduce the smarting on her back and thought, I shall run away, I shall get help from someone in another village and seek council from them.

She thought of the young boy Mihko who visited her village to trade his wares. She liked him and his gentle manner, his shyness when he spoke to her. As a young boy Mihko was attacked by a hyena and was left with a twisted leg, which caused him to limp when he walked. He was often ridiculed by the young girls in his village and were surprised when Kefhilwe befriended him, would talk to him and share her food with him on visits with her father when he came to trade his weaves in his village.

Mihko's family were of the light skinned hunter gatherers and Mihko as a hunter was thought well of in his village, especially for his bravery in tracking the Cheetah and setting traps.

THE RUNAWAYS

Kefhilwe waited till the moon was down and slipped away into the dark night carrying some dried meat and water for her travels. She avoided the usual route to the other village and finally arrived just before the dawn, at the rear of Mihko's hut.

It was fortunate that Mihko's hut was on the outskirts of the village close to his hunting ground and away from prying eyes. 'Mihko! Mihko! cried Kefhilwe. There was a moment and then a movement in the hut. Suddenly Mihko's head appeared in the opening and gasped, 'What on earth are you doing here?

'Let me come in and I will explain,' replied Kefhilwe. 'I cannot,' replied Mihko, news travels that you are promised to your cousin Bakang.' That is what I wish to speak to you about,' she replied, 'I cannot possibly form a union with him when I belong to another.' 'Another! Cried Mihko 'and who would that be?

'Oh, don't be foolish Mihko, I have thought of nothing else since I left my village, I know you like me and I have often seen you look away when I look up and you pretend you wasn't looking at me, It's you I want to spend all my days with, you I want to form a union with for always.' She was now crying wringing her hands together.

Mihko, with eyes bright, held out his hands to her and drew her into the hut. They sat together on Mihko's straw bed, holding each other's hands. 'Your family will already be looking for you, by now, so we will have to decide what to do.' exclaimed Mihko.

'Let us runaway and hide in the bush until I am with child.' she replied. Mihko, blushed and lowering his head, said, 'You are really serious about this aren't you? 'It's the only way, it is our tradition that they cannot possibly come between the union of a man and a woman, it's the law,' replied Kefhilwe. 'It is true what they say about you, a girl beyond her years,' he said laughingly.

Mihko collected his knives and basket weave shoulder bag. He lifted his long bow from the wall and releasing the gut, straddled it across his shoulder. He then rolled his straw blanket and tied it across Kefhilwe's shoulder.

'Come,' he said, 'follow my steps and stay close to me at all times.' 'But where can we go? They are sure to find us,' she replied. 'We are going deep into the bush, even your tribesmen would not dare enter, where we are going, for fear of getting lost.'

Mihko, stepped stealthy out of the hut and raising his arm, slowly beckoned Kefhilwe to follow. They stooped low and skirting the village were far into the bush as the sun had risen.

'We will have to travel fast to be at the water hole before the sun is too high and then on to my secret resting place close to the desert,' he told Kefhilwe. She looked at him with eyes shining and said, 'Oh Mihko, I knew you were meant for me, even the birds sang to me about you and the wind and the rain agreed, I just hope you will not invite trouble from my tribe and family.'

Mihko lowered his eyes and as if talking to his hands, said, 'Kefhilwe, I have taken you for my own, in our tribe, that is all that matters. If Bakang and your family come for you, I say, let them come and raising his bow, added, 'they will get what they deserve.'

Mihko was a fine hunter and when he caught game, it was only to supply their needs, nothing more; it was part of hunter gatherer's law. Kefhilwe kept a small fire burning in the cave and spent a lot of the time collecting wood. She would sit on a small rock outside the cave and patiently wait for Mihko's return. On his return they would sit together outside the cave with a small fire lighting their faces. As night closed in they would retire to the cave and lay together on Mihko's straw blanket, huddled together like two sleeping children.

Mihko had counted the moon traversing the night sky five times and decided it was time to return to his village. Kefhilwe was showing signs of being with child and Mihko would collect herbs which he would boil and make her drink to stop her being sick. One evening they were sat outside the cave and Kefhilwe said, 'You have been quiet these past sunsets, have I said something that troubles you? Mihko smiled and said, 'No, of course not, it is just time we returned to my village and confront our elders, that's all and it has been troubling me.' Kefhilwe just nodded in silence and retiring to the cave collected their belongings, for the journey the next dawn.

Mihko was awake before Kefhilwe and looking at her gently breathing, whispered, 'Kefhilwe, it is time we should be leaving.' Kefhilwe sat up and stretching her arms high, said, 'I shall never forget this time we have had together Mihko and if they do try to separate us, they can never take that from us, can they? Mihko smiled and replied, 'Who is the foolish one now, of course they cannot separate us, I swear by the little heartbeat you can feel from our child inside you.'

Kefhilwe, grinned and replied, 'Let's go!

THE CHEETAH RUN

They travelled two sunsets, making the journey slow to accommodate Kefhilwe's condition. The next morning early, Mihko told Kefhilwe he had decided to visit her family first and settle any outstanding account with her parents and Bakang. They were nearing the outskirts of her village when a shrill sound could be heard of women ululating. 'The Cheetah run,' exclaimed Mihko.

The Cheetah run was a tradition passed down through many generations of the tribes. Whenever a Cheetah was spotted worrying the cattle or attacking the small fowl they would prepare for this event. The purpose of the Cheetah run, involved the men folk and their young son's who would set a trap by enticing the Cheetah into the clearing where they would spear and kill it. The young girls of the tribe would cut long saplings from the hardened gnarled trees and fashion them into whips to be used on the young men to punish them for acts of cowardice, who failed to compete in the Cheetah run. Mihko told

Kefhilwe to stay close to him but always at his rear and not to make any sudden movements.

They reached the clearing and could see a man on horseback challenging the Cheetah with a long spear 'My uncle,' cried Kefhilwe. Her cousin Bakang was running away from the encounter calling the other young men to run with him to entice the Cheetah.

Kefhilwe's uncle's horse reared and threw him to the ground, the horse quickly getting to its feet and rearing tried to stamp on the Cheetah. This gave Kefhilwe's uncle time to flee. The Cheetah roared and sank its teeth into the horse's ankle, the horse falling to the ground. The horse struggled to its feet and limped away from the Cheetah. The Cheetah quickly turned and with the scent of blood in its nostrils started into a trot and then into a run towards Kefhilwe's uncle in the distance.

Kefhilwe stood frozen, holding Mihko's arm. 'Stay calm, I have in him in my sight, do not be afraid,' he said, reassuringly. Kefhilwe's uncle was in state of panic as he fled the Cheetah, the Cheetah quickly gaining ground on him. Kefhilwe's uncle realising that death was certain called to his family giving orders of bequests of his possessions after his demise.

In a moment Bakang and the young men had run passed Mihko and Kefhilwe, her uncle trailing behind. The Cheetah speeded up and nearing its prey sprang up to pounce on him.

Quickly, Mihko, dropped to his knee and drawing his bow to its full extent, fired the arrow at the Cheetah, piercing its neck. The Cheetah stopped in its flight, its body twisting fell to the ground.

Mihko quickly drew his long spear and with all his might plunged it into the heart of the Cheetah. The Cheetah stiffened and was still.

Kefhilwe's uncle was lying on the ground sobbing with relief and Kefhilwe, feeling pity for him kneeled and tried to lift him. Kefhilwe's uncle seeing her condition, exclaimed, 'No, my child it is I that should help you.'

Bakang seeing the situation confronted Mihko, and hesitating fell to his knees and thanked him for saving his father's life. The womenfolk ululated and shouted, 'Kefhilwe has returned to the tribe with her husband warrior.'
Bakang looked at them both and grinning put him arms over their shoulders, led them back to the clearing.

THE TRIAL

The following morning Kefhilwe and Mihko were called from the visitor's hut where they slept, to attend the Kgotla and stand trial for their disobedience to their tribes. The dikgosi, leaders of both tribes sat on two straw high chairs, while the rest of the peoples sat in a circle below them. The families of both Kefhilwe and Mihko sat separate to each other.

The testifiers, for and against were sat together in front of the dikgosi. They were then both called to the centre of the open hut and made to stand in the middle. Kefhilwe and Mihko were called to sit next to them. A small wooden stool was brought for Kefhilwe to acknowledge her condition.

Kefhilwe's paternal aunt was to testify against her, while Bakang's father was to testify in favour of them. The kgosi from Mihko's tribe stood and called for the paternal aunt to come forward and state her case.

The damning indictment that ensued was to have witnesses testify to Kefhilwe's abnormal behaviour sighting cases of her talking to birds and animals alike and bewitching the boy Mihko. The paternal aunt stated cases very early on in Kefhilwe's life of being possessed of evil spirits. In the summing up she proclaimed that Kefhilwe should be sent into exile.

The kgosi from Mihko's tribe called on Bakang's father to state his case. Bakang's father stood up and exclaimed, 'I know nothing of these claims against my niece Kefhilwe. I have always found her a pleasant and gifted child and now a beautiful young woman with child. I should have been honoured to have had her for my daughter-in-law, but that is now never to be ' and looking at her, added 'She seems to have taken care of that in her own way,' which brought light laughter from the kgotla.

Composing himself, he added, 'Never the less, she has brought disgrace to both tribes, even though what she has done is not against both our laws and she has every right to proclaim who she wishes to spend the rest of her life with.'

He paused and then said, 'I suggest that the idea of exile should be dropped and we should welcome her husband warrior to our tribe, but not before, charging him ten cows and a bull, for impregnating my brother's daughter, in the manner in which it has been done.' He then turned to the paternal aunt and raising his hands, sat down.

The paternal aunt was quickly on her feet and cried, 'I warn you that this girl is possessed and should be banished from our tribe, no good will ever come from this union and my son should have been allowed to make his rightful claim to her.' The dikgosi both looked at Bakang and feeling he should say something, stood up and looking at Kefhilwe, said, 'I have no claim on Kefhilwe and if I had, I now relinquish all claims to her now' and sat back down again. 'This is a conspiracy,' cried the paternal aunt and stormed out of the open hut.

Both chiefs spoke together and the chief for Mihko's tribe stood up and proclaimed, 'So be it then, Mihko has inherited the parents of Kefhilwe and may their lives be both fruitful and long' and sat back down again. Kefhilwe and Mihko both stood and embraced each other. Bakang's father held Mihko by the shoulders and said, 'Welcome, I shall forever be in your debt for saving me from the Cheetah.' Bakang stood next to his father and added, 'Come Mihko we have to build a hut and make your wife comfortable and prepare for your firstborn.'

The baby gave out a whimpering cry, then a loud yell. Mihko stood outside the hut, when two women folk suddenly appeared carrying wet towels and large wooden bowls. Kefhilwe's mother poked her head out of the hut and beckoned Mihko to the entrance.

She looked at him and exclaimed, 'It's a boy! a fine healthy son, Kefhilwe is well, but tired, go now and give the good news to your family.' Mihko, eyes filled with tears, held both her hands and shook them up and down, saying, 'Oh, thank you mother, thank you!

Mihko was kept away from the hut for many moons and all men and boys were not allowed near her or the hut. Only, Kefhilwe's mother was allowed to attend to her. Her mother did everything for her, preparing her meals, washing the child, mixing special herbs for her to drink.

Kefhilwe spent all her days lying on her stomach eating porridge and drinking goat's milk. Her evenings were occupied holding the child and singing to him. 'Tuelo, Tuelo, my first born, you are a delight to my eyes.' she would say, 'Soon we will venture out and meet your father and all your cousins and added, 'I shall show you all your brothers and sisters of the sky and we will learn their songs together and get to know them well.'

Early one morning, Mihko was called to the hut, when it was bright and the day was still cool. They placed a stool for him to sit on; the family were gathered behind him.

Kefhilwe appeared at the entrance to the hut with Tuelo held high across her shoulder. 'Come Mihko,' she said shyly, 'come and meet your son'.

Mihko, approached Kefhilwe, slowly walking around her. 'What is the matter Mihko? asked Kefhilwe. Mihko kept walking and finally stopping, replied, 'You look different, you don't look like the Kefhilwe I know.'

Kefhilwe laughing said, 'It's because I am a mother now and have been made big with porridge and goats milk.' Mihko laughed with her and started to make a dance around Kefhilwe and his son Tuelo. The women joined in the celebration, ululating and swirling their shawls in a circle around the couple.

Bakang killed a goat and the celebrations lasted throughout the night till the early morning; Kefhilwe, Mihko and Tuelo had long since retired to their hut and were curled in a circle fast asleep.

REPRISE

And so the story of the death and life of Kefhilwe now returns to the beginning, when creation spoke with her. And concludes with the grown man Tuelo carrying his mother Kefhilwe to her resting place next to where Mihko had been laid this long time past. Stories would be told of Kefhilwe for many years to come and tell how one small gifted girl's trust in life would be passed down through generations.

5

SINS OF THE FATHER

THE INTERVIEW

A tall, wide window, open, looked out on to a large bay, where small sailing crafts, tilted, clung to the mud at low tide. In the far distance a loaded freighter gave off its final two whoops, before heading for foreign lands. In the large vaulted room, the autumn sun cast shadows across the Mother Superior's desk. She studied the last file of the day. The Novice was the last student teacher today to be interviewed for the post of Religious Instruction, which had become vacant, with Sister Alberta's retirement. She flicked through the pages and stopped at her family background. Her family were of the old shipping class and still held important posts in the Capital. She rang a small brass bell and in a moment a Sister swung open the door, briskly ushering the Novice into the room, before, quickly retiring, closing the door gently, behind her.

The Novice was a tall, slim girl, with a pale complexion, who stood nervously, with both hands clutching a shoulder bag in front her. The Mother Superior looked up and gestured her to the chair in front of the desk. The Novice sat down and lowered her eyes. She continued looking through the Novice's file until, closing it; she looked up and asked, 'Sister Agnese, I have noted from your file that you have excelled in all your subjects at the Ecclesiastical College. You came top of your class in Religious Instruction and have already been unconditionally offered a post at the prestigious, Our Lady of Mount Carmen's School for Girls, yet you come here today seeking a place at The Saint Paul's Seaman's Mission for the Poor. Don't you think your services would be better spent and furthermore, appreciated at Our Lady's, rather than here?

The Novice seemed to wince, but straightened up and said gently. 'Quite the opposite Mother Superior, you see, if I were to ask Jesus the same question, I know what His answer would be. No, as a servant of Jesus, my place is to serve Him unconditionally and there is no better place that could I serve Him than at the Mission.' The Mother Superior, gave a bemused smile and added, 'That is all very well, Sister Agnese, but the reality of it is, you will not find it an easy task dealing with these children who come from sometimes, troubled, if not violent family backgrounds. Most of these children are special needs and require special attention, which would need all your patience, love and care.' She opened the file at her family background and pointing to it and asked, 'Do you think, considering your gentile background you will be able to cope with these difficult tasks?

The Novice looked up from her hands and answered calmly, 'I think I can answer that question quite simply, Mother Superior, you see, when I decided to take the vows, I knew my life would not be easy, having decided to live a separate life apart from others and devoting my life to Jesus; and His place was always with the poor, I can think of no better place that I could fulfil that devotion, than at the Mission.' The Mother Superior closed the file and looking up said to the Novice, 'The interview is now over, we will be in touch with you, when we have completed interviewing all the applicants. Good day, Sister.'

SAINT PAUL'S SEAMAN'S MISSION FOR THE POOR

Sister Agnese was unpacking her belongings and setting them in the large chest of drawers next to her bedside. She was happy with herself and was looking forward to visiting the Saint Paul's Mission and meet her new class and be introduced to the children. She lifted the heavy crucifix from the suitcase and kissed the feet of Jesus on the cross, before placing it on her bedside cabinet, near her pillow. She thought of the letter when it had arrived from the Mission and on opening it, read that she was offered the post of Religious Instructor at the Mission. It was only provisional of course, but that did not matter to her, because she knew that with Jesus's help she would prevail. She straightened the bed covers and turned to look out through her small window onto the bay. The sun was bright even for an autumn day. She could see two large freighters way out in the roads waiting for the tide and the small sailing crafts bobbing to and fro on their moorings in the bay.

She thought of her father, a captain in the Merchant navy and the long periods when he would be away at sea. She shuddered involuntary and screwing her eyes tight tried not to remember the incidents when her father would quietly enter her bedroom late at night and in the moonlight she would see his large round white face perspiring with eyes glaring. He would smile and gently lift the bedclothes and touch her. She would try to resist and say to him, 'No daddy, I don't like it! He would put his finger to his lips and say, 'Hush, my dear, this will be our little secret.'

She stared at the crucifix on the bedside cabinet for a while and then dropped to her knees by the bedside. 'Oh! Blessed Jesus,' she cried, 'help me today to serve you! Let your blessed spirit pass through me and help my dear little children in class today! She crossed herself, and kissed the small crucifix which hung from here neck.

There came a gentle tap on the door and the Mother Superior entered, saying, 'Your class is now waiting for you, Sister Agnese.' The Novice stood up and quickly followed the Mother Superior down the dark corridor. 'Your class! she repeated to herself! How wonderful! she thought. They passed a small chapel leading to the left of the corridor and the Mother Superior paused and said, 'You may use this chapel for your quiet times,' Sister. 'Yes!, Yes ! Thank you, Mother Superior,' replied the Novice. They passed through the kitchen where other Novices were, heads bowed, busy, cleaning up after the breakfast meal. They passed along another corridor and were suddenly out onto the courtyard. The sun was dazzling and the Novice shaded her eyes from the glare of the sun. 'Come now,' ordered the Mother Superior and strode across the courtyard to the main entrance to the school. Above the archway was an inscription, which read, Before ye seek to enter, become as little children

'Oh! Mother Superior,' exclaimed the Sister, 'what wonderful words and so appropriate.' The Mother Superior let the remark pass and ushered the Sister through the school entrance into the dimly lit corridor. They walked past several classrooms the children busy writing in their books, whilst the teacher wrote on the blackboard. At the fourth classroom the door was open and the Mother Superior looked over the frosted glass and saw the children, sat silent with arms folded. 'After you, Sister,' said the Mother Superior.

THE CLASSROOM

Sister Agnese straightened herself and walked quickly into the classroom. The classroom was quite large, with rows of desks each side, leaving walkways down the middle and each side. Frosted panes of glass ran each side of the walls to add some privacy to the lessons. The Headmistress stood near the desk, smiled at the Sister, and said, 'Welcome Sister,' and turning to the class, said loudly, 'Now children, pay attention please, I would like you to meet your new teacher, this is Sister Agnese, so let us all give her a warm welcome please.' The children chorused, 'Good morning Sister Agnese.' The Novice beamed, and replied, 'Well good morning to you, my dear, darling little children.' A few sniggers appeared from the back of the class and the Headmistress, said loudly, 'Now! That will do! The Mother Superior walked across the classroom to the Head-mistress and said to the Novice, 'This is Sister Dolas, should you wish to ask any questions regarding your position at the school, she is quite capable of answer-ing them.' 'Oh, thank you Mother Superior, I will, I will,' gushed the Novice.

'Very good,' said the Mother Superior, now Sister Dolas will acquaint you with the rules and regulations of the school and ensure you settle in as quickly as possible' and added, 'These children have fallen behind in their studies, due to Sister Alberta's retirement and I expect you Sister Agnese, to get the children back on path, before their end of term exams.' 'Yes, of course,' said the Novice, 'I will do my utmost to attain that goal.' 'Very good, I shall now leave you for further instruction from the Headmistress, Sister Dolas.'

The rest of the morning was taken up with the timetables and subject mate-rial for Religious Studies. Sister Agnese, carefully cut out little white cards with which the children could write their first names and place them on their desk, so the Sister could remember them. The children were delighted with the task given them and became quite noisy, chatting to each other and showing each other, their cards. 'That will quite do,' said Sister Dolas, loudly. 'Oh! I don't mind at all,' said the Novice, 'I love to see children being playful and enjoying themselves.'

Sister Dolas turned and said to the Novice, 'That may be all very well, but these children will be quick to take advantage of your generosity,' said the Headmistress. The Novice smiled shyly and lowered her eyes. She added, 'I shall leave you for the last half hour before lunch and allow you to get better ac-quainted with your class.' 'Thank you Headmistress,' said the Novice, walking her to the door and closing it behind her. 'Better acquainted with your class! she repeated to herself and smiled joyfully.

Just then, a cry was heard to come from the back of the class. 'Give it back to me! Give it back to me! Tommy Driscoll,' came the voice. A young girl stood up and said, 'Sister Agnese, Tommy Driscoll has spat on my card and tore it up! Sister Agnese frowned and walked slowly down the middle aisle to where a pretty little girl with clothes threadbare stood. 'What is your name?' asked the Novice. 'Mary Walsh,' replied the little girl.' 'Well, Mary Walsh,' said the Novice, go and sit at the front of the class and I shall attend to this.' The Novice turned and looked down at Tommy Driscoll, a dishevelled untidy boy with broken teeth and asked, 'Now Tommy, what made you treat little Mary in such an unkind way?

Tommy squirmed in his seat and slouching back, said contemptuously, 'Yea! well she said I didn't spell my name properly on the card, so I showed her what, eh? and then sneered and laughed out loud, looking around the class for approval. 'Miss! Miss! Sister Agnese turned to a rather big boy for the class and said, 'yes? The big boy said, 'My name is Liam Latchford Miss, and it is not really that, you see, Constable Walsh, Mary's father caught Tommy Driscoll's father, red handed, breaking in the Ship Chandlers Store and stealing blankets and ship's stores. His family hate the Walsh's.'

'It's not true! Shouted Tommy Driscoll, 'my father is at sea on a long voyage. Anyway, you should, not be in this class Latchford, It's only because you failed your exams last year, that you have to stay down, You Dunderhead! 'Now! Now! That will quite do, Tommy Driscoll,' said the Novice. 'Now, I want you to go to the blackboard and write ten times, I must be kind to my school friends.' Tommy slunk back in his seat and slowly shook his head. 'Oh! That's a laugh sister, shouted one of the boys at the front of the class. 'And why is that? Enquired the Novice. 'Because he can't write! chorused the class and broke out into peals of laughter and started banging the desks.

Tommy grinned through broken teeth and jeered, 'You see Sister! This is my classroom and I will do what I like and neither you nor anyone can stop me, see! 'Tommy Driscoll for teacher,' they all chanted. He looked around the classroom laughing loudly, enjoying the attention he was getting from the children. 'Stop! Oh! Stop! Please,' said the Novice, raising her voice. 'Tommy Driscoll! To the Headmistress's office now!

IN THE CHAPEL

Sister Agnese often came to the chapel for quiet times and prayer. It was quite a small chapel in size with two tiny cloisters each side of the altar. A large crucifix hung above the altar, with a life size Jesus hanging, looking down at His disciples. The Novice stood in awe of the image and often came to touch the feet of Jesus. She would pray ardently for hours on end and would sometimes fall asleep in prayer. It was such a wonderful feeling; she thought to be so close to the image of her saviour. It was an escape, no a refuge, she thought. The weeks had turned into months and it was now only two weeks before Christmas. She thought of Tommy Driscoll and remembered his father was being paroled out of jail for the Christmas. The threats and the taunts had never stopped, but they were more in the way of looks of contempt and sneers.

Today, Sister Agnese sat in the small chapel, quite alone. She thought of the incident in the classroom that first morning and sighed. If only I could have been more understanding and loving to that poor innocent boy, she thought, after all, he is only a child. I should have been more gracious and loving, she had thought, but no, it only made matters worse and angered him. He seemed to draw strength from her kindness. She sat up from kneeling and rubbing her knees, rested her back against the wooden seat panelling. How peaceful it was, she thought and closed her eyes. A slight stirring sound came from the back of the altar and she quickly opened her eyes. She looked up at the face of Jesus on the cross for reassurance and much to her fright; He appeared to smile down at her. No! No! That can't be,' she cried. His angelic face continued to smile down on her and He slowly, began to remove the nails from each hand, before stepping down and began walking towards her. 'Oh! My God,' she cried, 'heaven help me, this can't be happening! His angelic face suddenly began to twist into grotesque features, first it was Tommy Driscoll, sneering at her and then the face of her father, the large round white face perspiring with eyes glaring. The face then turned bright red and horns appeared at each temple. 'The Devil! She cried. He was now leaning over her, his fetid breath made her turn her face away from him and she screamed out at the top of her voice.

A loud knock on the door of the Novice's bedroom resounded in the night. 'Sister Agnese? Sister Agnese? Are you alright? came the voice of the Mother Superior. 'Yes! Yes! Answered the Novice. 'Good grief, you were screaming at the top of your voice,' she added. 'Yes! I must have been dreaming,' she exclaimed, 'but I am alright now, thank you, for your concern.'

She was bathed in sweat and turned to look at the crucifix on the bedside cabinet. It was the luminous type and glowed in the dark; she shuddered, put the bedside lamp on and jumped out of bed. She felt much calmer and drew the small curtain across the window. The sky was ink black with bright star dust strewn across the night sky. A half crescent moon hung just above the sea, while a small pilot boat chugged slowly across the bay.

CHRISTMAS WEEK

A small Christmas tree stood in the corner of the classroom. The children had spent the past week decorating it and Sister Agnese, carefully placed a tiny figure of an angel at the top of the tree. They wrapped empty boxes with Christmas paper from the kitchen, to give the impression that presents were beneath the tree. The children folded coloured crepe paper into concertina shapes and festooned them around Sister Agnese's desk.

It was mid-morning and the children were busy with preparations for their end of term exams. Sister Agnese sat at her desk reading from her bible and looking up was happy to see that life in the classroom had finally settled down. Tommy Driscoll was unusually quiet. He was lifting his desk a fraction to let his classmate, peak under to see what he was hiding. The Novice decided to ignore it and thought it best to stay away from any confrontation with him.

She cleared her throat and said, 'Now children the rest of this morning is going to be taken up with, The Story of Jesus,' she smiled. The children shouted, 'Hurray! Mary Walsh raised her hand and asked, 'Will it be about the baby Jesus and His being born in a manger, Sister? She smiled and said, 'Yes, Mary, that is what I want to talk about and discuss with the class,' she answered. There was a loud guffaw from the back of the classroom and someone shouted, 'Oh! No! not that old codswallop again! Sister Agnese put her bible down and could feel her temper rising, but said calmly, 'Is that what you consider the Story of Jesus is all about, Tommy Driscoll? 'Who said I said anything Sister' and laughed loudly, turning towards Mary Walsh, sticking his tongue out and blowing a raspberry. 'That will quite do for now, Tommy Driscoll, now you know what happened the last time you went before the headmistress, don't you?

'Yea! Well that won't happen again see, because my father is home from sea now and he promised to come and sort you out proper.'

Sister Agnese, stood up and felt a little dizzy, but steadying herself against the desk, she said curtly, 'Now that is quite foolish Tommy, isn't it, you know quite well as the whole class does that your father was only released from jail, two days ago, on parole, I believe, just for Christmas, wasn't it? she said slyly. She gasped and thought, 'Oh! Blessed Jesus, what have I said, realising she had allowed herself to be provoked. 'Not true! Not true! Screamed Tommy Driscoll. 'You're all against us, the whole bloody lot of you! Bloody bunch of Holy rollers, me dad calls you! Bloody hypocrites! Who says your bloody Jesus was ever born anyway, he says, there is no bloody proof! All that bloody bullshit about him dying on the cross and coming alive again! Where's your bloody proof, that's what my dad wants to know,' he laughed loudly, turning and expecting a response from the class. A simple faraway smile broke out on Sister Agnese's face and she could feel her lips begin to tremble and steadying herself, with her hands behind her back, she started to slowly walk down the mid-aisle towards Tommy Driscoll. 'Now Tommy, I think you have said quite enough, for the day. I am taking you to the Headmistress's office, but this time you will not be coming back to this class ever! She emphasised. 'You're not taking me anywhere, Sister! He shouted. I warned you before! Now! You are going to get it!

'He's got a gun! Shouted Liam Latchford. Tommy, grinning through broken teeth, raised his desk top and produced a large revolver and pointing it at the Novice said, 'You've been asking for this for a long time Sister, now see if your bloody Jesus is going to help you! The Novice continued to walk slowly towards Tommy. 'I'm warning you Sister! Come a step closer and I'll blow your bloody head off! 'Now, Tommy, don't be foolish,' she smiled 'and put that gun away.' Sister Agnese, was now just a few feet away from Tommy and her face suddenly broke out into a smile of recognition. At last! She thought, her prayers had been answered, that was it! She knew the answer! Jesus had fulfilled His promise!

Just then a shot rang out, echoing down the hallway.

SINS OF THE FATHER

The white van arrived late in the afternoon and two men in white coats carried a folded stretcher through the corridor, past the kitchen and stood outside the chapel. 'Wait here,' the Mother Superior told the orderlies. 'You will not need that stretcher; I shall go and fetch her.' She turned to the other two nuns and putting her two finger to her lips, whispered. 'Come!

As they walked towards Sister Agnese's room a voice echoed through the corridors, they could still hear her shrill, wailing voice, laughing hysterically, as she raved. 'It is not their fault at all, they are just sweet little children of Jesus, innocent little babies of Christ!

It's the sins of the father, that is to blame, yes the sins of the father! she screamed.

6

MR. WINTHROP (GOD'S JESTER)

EARLY RETIREMENT

Mr. Winthrop's study was quite small, but carried a vaulted ceiling with low wooden beams, straddling the walls. A warm summer breeze blew through the open patio doors, lifting the chintz curtains, onto his old desk which faced his long garden. The walls were lined with books shelves, with an old fashioned pair of wooden steps, open near the door. His desk chair was of the swivel type with casters. The typewriter click clacked slowly, as if someone was typing with one finger. Mr. Winthrop, squinted through his thick lensed glasses and slowly shaking his head, grabbed the sheet of paper from the typewriter and through it into the basket near his desk.

'Charles! his wife called from the dining room. 'Are you going to spend all day, clickety clacking on that bloody typewriter? 'your dinner is on the table, going cold again and I cannot spend all day preparing meals for you, just to end up throwing them in the bin! Mr. Winthrop sighed and lifting his glasses on to his head, pushed his desk chair back and replied, 'Coming dear.'

Mrs Winthrop was a large breasted woman with flabby arms. Her blond hair had turned prematurely silver grey and her countenance carried an air of haughtiness. 'Sit down Charles,' she commanded. They both sat quietly eating their meal, while Mrs Winthrop swiftly demolished her sausage and mash and delicately wiping her mouth with her napkin, asked, 'Did the newspaper finally agree on the terms of your early retirement pension?

Mr Winthrop raised his head from his meal and replied quietly, 'Yes, but they are only going to pay my pension from the time I finished my apprenticeship, which will be a total of thirty five years,' he said.

'What! The bloody rogues,' she exclaimed. 'You have spent the best part of your life as Copy editor with the Chronicle and this is how they decide to treat you after such loyal service, It is a bloody disgrace, it is, a bloody disgrace,' she added. 'Well, what can you expect, the Union doesn't have the same clout as it used to,' he replied. 'Bloody Union! she continued, 'just a bunch of sodding Communists that is all they were, a load of bloody reds.'

'Well they did a lot of good in the old days and helped a great deal in getting us better living conditions, why we could have never afforded to buy this house and send Mavis to a decent school if it had not been for the Union,' he argued.

'Well, just tell me Charlie, how are we going to afford to live with that meagre pension? And you will not be entitled to your State Pension for another nine years,' she added. Mr Winthrop, put down his knife and fork and smiling said, 'I was thinking of finishing that novel I started writing and maybe getting it published.'

Mrs Winthrop was taking a sip of water from her glass and blurted out, 'What! And putting her glass carefully down on the table, began to chuckle to herself and quickly picking up her napkin, holding it to her mouth, started to shake uncontrollably, whilst laughing into her napkin. 'Oh dear, Charles,' she finally said, 'are you serious? Do you really think anyone would be interested in reading your novel?, she asked and added, 'you have been writing it for the past twenty five years' and sniggered, 'it will probably be well past its sell by date by now.' 'Well I can only try,' he replied, defensively. 'Well, in the meanwhile, I shall speak to my old employer, who I worked for, during the time you were on strike and see if he can offer me some part-time work to keep us going while we are waiting to get your book published, although I won't hold my breath,' she laughed.

A GODLY MAN

Mr Winthrop sat at his desk, staring at his typewriter and thought, I bought this typewriter when I had just finished my apprenticeship, god that seems a long time ago, he mused. He looked across at his pile of manuscript and considered re-reading the last two pages of the last chapter. This was a device he often used to keep the storyline going, especially when he was stuck on an issue of development. Oh what's the use, he thought, maybe my wife is right, it feels like an uphill battle to finish this book and maybe I will never get anyone to publish it. He felt a sudden pang of regret as if he was now ready to admit defeat and thought of the long hours he had wasted writing the book. He thought of his wife and her mocking eyes and her treating him with derision. He felt weak and apathetic and placing his head on his hands closed his eyes.

He sat with his eyes closed for what seemed an age and feeling like he was at the very bottom of a deep pit, with darkness all around him, he shivered and cried out in desperation, 'Oh God, please help me, I do so want to become a writer and write books, I would give anything, anything,' he sobbed. He raised his head and looking up, as if waiting to see if his prayer had been answered, but everything was still. 'Oh! I am just kidding myself,' he said out loud and placed his head back down on his hands and closed his eyes.

Suddenly, there came a gust of wind which blew in from the garden, forcing the study doors ajar and looking up in astonishment, could see a bright illumination, lighting up his study. His manuscript on top of his desk flew up in the air. It was if a blast of pure spirit was blowing around him and through him and the feeling of some magnificent presence all around him. 'Oh my God, what is happening ! he cried.

As quickly, as it started, the wind dropped and the room returned to its former light. Mr. Winthrop sat transfixed, not believing what had happened, but for the first in his adult life, had a feeling of complete calmness and confidence. Slowly, a great weariness overcame him and in half doubt slowly shook his head in disbelief. He wanted terribly to sleep and placing his head on his hands again, closed his eyes and passed into a state of complete exhaustion.

'Charles! Charles! His wife called loudly. 'Where are you? Mr Winthrop stirred from his lethargy and answered, 'yes, dear I am in the study.' He looked up and saw his manuscript was strewn around his desk and covered the floor near his seat. The study doors were ajar and his wife appeared from the garden and exclaimed, 'Have you gone completely mad? Look at the state of the place, what on earth have you been up to?

Mr Winthrop, with a vacant expression on his face, scratching his head, said, 'I am not sure, I think I must have fallen asleep and there must have been a strong wind which blew the study doors open and scattered my manuscript everywhere,' he concluded. 'Nonsense! Utter nonsense,' his wife exclaimed, 'it has been one of the calmest days we have had all summer. Is this just another way of admitting your complete failure as a writer,' she queried and added, 'I always told you to number your manuscript and now you are going to have a devilish time putting this lot in order.' Mr Winthrop looked up and replied, 'I have decided not to finish the book, it is a load of rubbish anyway, the content is weak and there is little continuity,' he added.

'Well, it is about time you came to your senses and started facing reality,' she said, 'staying in this study morning, noon and night has softened your brain, now we can start looking to getting you a proper job and get all this nonsense about writing a book completely out of your head,' she said finally.

Mr Winthrop, turned on his swivel chair and glaring at his wife, said, firmly, 'I am not giving up writing, quite the contrary, I have decided to write a trilogy, a period piece that covers three generations of a family, the idea came to me suddenly whilst I was resting earlier. I am going to call it, The Family from the North Country, it will have drama and romance with plenty of intrigue,' he added.

Mrs Winthrop face went a bright red and blurted, 'You have gone completely mad' and laughing loudly, said, 'I think there must be three generations of madness in your family and it has finally got to you.' I do not believe what I am hearing' and added, 'when are you going to write this War and Peace epic? She queried.

'Right now,' Mr Winthrop replied and commenced to pick up his manuscript, pushing it into the straw basket near his desk.

THE MOVING FINGER WRITES

The hall clock chimed and struck three. Mr Winthrop sharpened his last pencil and placed it in the holder. He pushed his typewriter away from him and carefully stacked his new manuscript into a neat pile and placed them in front of him. He took a sharpened pencil from the holder and pausing, wrote, The Family from the North Country, Chapter one, Part one, A Family in Crisis at the top of the page and began to write. He felt exhilarated and puzzled at how easy and effortlessly the words began to flow and wondered why he had laboured so long in the past. He wrote furiously and marvelled at the speed in which he wrote. The words seemed to come naturally, even magically and creatively onto the manuscript.

He was suddenly startled into hearing the hall clock strike ten and wrote page eighty-five, end of chapter one at the bottom of the page. He punched the manuscript and placed it into a folder. He opened a drawer in his desk and produced a large brown manila envelope and placing his completed manuscript inside, he sealed it and wrote on the front, Wainwright Publishing Company adding his address and telephone number on the back.

He stretched and yawned and placed the manila envelope back in his desk drawer. I shall post it tomorrow, special delivery and then thought, no, better still, I will deliver it myself personally and claim it as my intellectual property.

Mr Winthrop felt very tired but had a wonderful, satisfied feeling of accomplishment. He looked at his watch and said, 'Good gracious, is that the time? He pushed his swivel chair back and went to draw the study curtains. He looked out and could see a full moon, iridescent in the back night sky. Just then a comet flared across the horizon and as quickly disappeared into the night. Is that some kind of sign he thought and smiled to himself, but inwardly, thanked God for a wonderful day.

He climbed the stairs and after attending to his toiletry, quietly opened the bedroom door. 'Oh, you are still awake,' he said, to his wife. 'Yes,' she replied, 'I was wondering when you would be coming to bed, how is War and Peace coming on? she chortled. 'Oh, not bad, in fact I am quite pleased with what I have done today,' he answered. 'Well do let me know when you have completed the first twenty pages, won't you, so I can be the first to read your sojourn,' she mused. 'Oh, I have completed Chapter one already today and have decided to take it to the publisher's tomorrow morning early, I must find out the best train to the Capital first thing,' he said to himself.

'I will believe that when I see it,' his wife, replied and sternly said, 'are you putting the light out then?

WAINWRIGHT PUBLISHING COMPANY

Mr Winthrop passed through the revolving doors of Wainwright Publishing Company and approaching the reception desk, stood waiting for the receptionist to finish talking on the phone. He held his manila envelope with his manuscript tightly under his arm and turning marvelled at the spacious entrance to the publishing company. Dotted around the reception area were several large round mahogany tables with books scattered on them and leather armchairs each side. Several people were sat talking, sat in the armchairs.

'Can I help you, sir? Mr Winthrop turned to face the receptionist, a tall, slim, blond young girl, with bright red lips. Mr Winthrop stuttered, 'Oh! Y, yes, you can, I should like to speak to someone, regarding a book I am writing and wished to have published,' he added.

The receptionist looked Mr Winthrop up and down and said smiling, 'Oh you do, do you? and added, 'I am afraid it is not as simple matter as you may think, a Mr?

'Winthrop, Charles Winthrop,' he replied. 'Well, Mr Charles Winthrop, you will notice several other visitors today with the same intention, sitting in the armchairs and they have been waiting several months applying, just to speak with an associate publisher, so you see, I am afraid you have had a wasted journey.' 'Oh, I see,' replied, Mr Winthrop, 'I did not realise that, but could I just hand it in over the counter and wait for a reply? he asked.

The receptionist appearing irritated, replied, 'I am sorry sir, but as I explained, you will have to go through the normal procedure, as everyone else did. There are application submission forms at the entrance to the lobby, which you can collect on your way out, good day, sir.' Mr Winthrop tipped his hat and said, 'Yes, yes, of course and thank you very much for all your help and advice.'

'Charlie! Charlie! It is you isn't it? A large gentleman with a moonlike face, holding a big cigar, patted Mr Winthrop on the shoulder and added, 'by jove it is you, Charlie Winthrop, don't you recognise me? It's Fred, Fred Burnley, we were at school together, why it must be all of forty years since we last set eyes on each other.'

'Fred Burnley, 'Well I'll be blowed,' said Mr Winthrop and asked, 'Fred, what are you doing here?

'I work here, have done so these past twenty five years, I am an associate publisher, come, come and sit down and tell me all that has been happening to you these past forty years' and turning to the receptionist, said, 'it's all right Miss Holmes, I shall attend to this matter, Oh, and could you kindly bring a pot of tea for two to my office at once.' The receptionist gave a bewildered look and replied, 'certainly sir, right away sir.'

'Well now, Charlie, do tell me all about what has been happening to you these past years? Fred Burnley, was sat behind his large desk, lighting a big cigar. Just then a gentle tap sounded on his door. 'Come in,' he commanded. The receptionist came in carrying a large tray with a silver tea set. 'Oh, yes, Geralyn, do put it on the table over there, would you my dear,' he said, pointing to the corner. The receptionist nodded, placed the large tray on the corner table and quietly closed the office door behind her.

Mr Winthrop sat in one of the large leather chairs next the associate publisher's desk, placing his manila envelope on top of it. Fred Burnley poured two cups of tea and carried the tray and placed it on the desk next to Mr Winthrop. 'Help yourself to the milk and sugar Charlie and come, tell me what you have been up to these past years?

Mr Winthrop took a sip of tea and said, 'Well Fred, first of all, I never in my wildest dreams expected to find you working in a publishing company.' and then proceeded to bring him up to date with his current situation. Fred Burnley listened attentively and finally replied, 'Well I knew after I left college that the newspaper lark was not for me, a bit too unpredictable, if you ask me,' he added and continued, 'so I went into publishing, oh it is not a bad business, had its ups and downs, but it has kept me busy, what? Fred Burnley, paused and then looking at the manila envelope on his desk, he said, 'The publishing business is having a bit of a hard time of it at the moment, what with all the new-fangled electronic stuff coming out on the market today' and added, 'I've always said, that the feel of a good book in the hands whilst reading can never be a substitute for all these new electronic devices.'

Mr Winthrop frowned and said, 'Well I was hoping that maybe someone could take a look at what I have written and at least give me a bit of advice, would be most helpful' and added, 'I think maybe my wife has been right all this time, telling me to get the notion of writing a book, let alone a trilogy, out of my head, is suddenly coming true.'

Mr Burnley smiled and said, 'hey cheer up Charlie, all is not lost, I can certainly get one of my juniors to give it the once over and get them to contact you, but it may take quite some time, you know, they have quite a backlog of submitted manuscripts to sift through' and added, 'I tell you what, let me put it near the top of the pile for you as a gesture of goodwill to help an old pal out, eh? 'That would be splendid,' replied Mr Winthrop and just then the telephone rang.

'Oh yes, put him through at once' and hand held over the receiver, said, 'listen Charlie, I have an important client on the line, would you let the receptionist let you out and keep smiling, eh!

MR WINTHROP?

'Charles! Charles! His wife called, 'that publishing company is on the phone again, I am putting them through to your study,' she said, angrily. Mr Winthrop was sat on his swivel chair with a huge pile of manuscript placed to the side of him. Picking up his phone he said, 'yes, Charles Winthrop speaking.'

'Oh, Mr Winthrop, I am so glad that I have manged to get hold of you, It is Geralyn, Geralyn Holmes, the receptionist, from Wainwright Publishing' and added, 'I had the pleasure of meeting you when you first came to our office.'. 'Oh, yes, I remember you Miss Holme, what can I do for you? he asked.

Miss Holmes, in a hurried voice, said, 'Alistair Wainwright jnr, our CEO has asked me to arrange a meeting with him, at your earliest convenience, that is.' 'Oh, this is a surprise,' he stated, 'would sometime towards the end of this week, be convenient? he asked. 'Shall we say, this Thursday, at 9.30 am, suit you, Mr Winthrop? 'Yes, yes, that will be fine,' he replied. 'Oh, and by the way, have you completed any more chapters of the first part of the trilogy? asked Miss Holmes.

Mr Winthrop, glanced at the pile of manuscript on his desk and replied, 'I have. In fact I am just concluding the first book,' he said, proudly.' 'Wonderful, Mr Winthrop, Mr Wainwright would be delighted if you could bring all of your completed work so far and added, 'Alistair asked me to convey his best wishes and looks forward to the meeting you.'

The phone clicked and Mr Winthrop, beaming, placed the phone back on the receiver.

'Mr Winthrop? So pleased to meet you',' said, Alistair Wainwright, smiling. Mr Winthrop was led into a large, spacious office, with a window that covered the whole of the opposite wall that overlooked the city centre. 'Yes, quite impressive, isn't it,' said the CEO, nodding to the large landscape window and waved Mr Winthrop to a large leather chair next to his polished mahogany desk. Fred Burnley was stood near the drinks cabinet and asked, 'what will you have Charlie? We've got the lot here, bourbon, whiskey, gin or just plain wine? he asked. 'Oh, nothing for me, it is much too early,' he answered. 'Well I am sure you will not mind me having one, how about you Alistair? he asked the CEO. 'No, I agree with Mr Winthrop, much too early in the day for that,' he replied.

Alistair Wainwright jnr, sat down behind his large mahogany desk and with open palms, said, 'Now, let us get down to business, shall we, Fred has shown me the first draft of your manuscript, which I am informed you intend to turn into a trilogy. Now I shall come straight to the point in that I am largely impressed with your work and can say quite categorically that I have not read such a fascinating piece of work since the likes of Amis or Golding and you may rightfully think that I am shooting myself in the foot, so to speak, by telling you all this, but to be quite frank, my dear sir, I should like you to consider our publishing company as a family run business and would warmly invite you to be a part of that family.'

'Mr Winthrop gasped and said, 'good god, I don't know what to say, this has come as a complete surprise to me.' 'Yes,' said the CEO, looking at Fred Burnley and smiling, added, 'you could say, it came as a complete surprise to us as well.'

AND HAVING WRIT MOVE ON

'I am very sorry but, Mr Drummond is not available for comment, right now, or for the foreseeable future. I am afraid and you will have to write to his personal assistant, Miss Holmes for an interview, but I am quite sure it will be a long wait, considering his work schedule.'

Geralyn Holmes replaced the receiver on the stand and smiled inwardly. She had arrived, so she thought and pondered, Personal Assistant to Charles Winthrop and then corrected herself, oh no, aka Sven Drummond the new voice of English literature, or so the critics named him.

She scanned his list of appointments and arrangements to be discussed, which were; the serialisation of his famous trilogy in a national newspaper, the film rights to be negotiated, book signings, television appearances, etc, etc.

To think, she thought, that this wonderful, wonderful man would turn out to be such an important influence in her life and just a short eighteen months ago when he first walked into Wainwright Publishing.

His trilogy was in its 4th printing and his new novel, The Derbyshire's which has sold out orders, even before publication. She marvelled at his sumptuous new apartment in the centre of the city and the wonderful cocktail parties thrown to celebrate his achievements.

She then frowned and thought of his wife, who had overshadowed all of his success, by throwing a fit and having a nervous breakdown on top of it all. How could she be so inconsiderate, she thought, still it is good that she is now out of the picture for a while, having been admitted to a private hospital for convalescing.

She bathed and put on her favourite perfume, finished her makeup, straightened her suit in the mirror and said out loud, 'right then, let's get to my goldmine, Sven' and called a cab to his apartment.

The doorbell chimed and moments later a smart young maid answered the door and said, 'Oh good evening Miss Holmes, do come in. Mr Drummond is just about ready, shall I tell him you are here? she asked. 'Uh, no, just carry on with what you are doing, I wish to surprise him,' she added.

Geralyn tapped on the bedroom door and said, 'Sven! May I come in? and entered the bedroom. Mr Winthrop, was stood in front of his large bedroom mirror in his silk dressing gown, tying his bow tie. 'These darn bow ties are a bloody nuisance trying to get them straight,' he exclaimed.

'Here, let me help you Charlie boy,' and holding her body close to him, smiled in his face and said, 'there! that should do it' and holding both his shoulders, drew him to her and kissed him hard on the mouth.

'Oh dear, now look what I have done,' she whispered, 'lipstick, I best remove it at once, we would not like to have people talking, now would we? And gave him a sly wink.

The doorbell chimed again and Mr Winthrop moved quickly away from Miss Holmes, adjusting his dressing gown and sat down at his dressing table. There was a gentle tap on the door and Geralyn said, 'come in!

Alistair Wainwright jnr in evening suit and white scarf, hailed, 'Ah! The man of the moment, or should I say, a man for all seasons, would be more apropos,' he added. Mr Winthrop, lowered his head and smiled. 'Are we all ready then? asked, Miss Holmes, feeling as though she had lost control of the situation, 'we had better hurry, if we are to make Sven's talk, about his new book, on time.'

A CALL FROM THE PRIVATE HOSPITAL

The large hotel conference room resounding to applause and cheers from the audience. Charles Winthrop aka Sven Drummond, nodded his head in appreciation and turning to Alistair Wainwright, shook his hand and sat down again. 'Wonderful, wonderful,' said Alistair Wainwright and thank you so much Sven for that exciting review of your forthcoming new book, The Derbyshire's' and I should like to add you have very cunningly left us wondering about the ending, as you so often did with your now classic trilogy, The Family from the North Country.

Turning to the audience he added, 'we shall now partake of some light refreshment before we proceed with Sven's questions about the new novel and may I add future novels, which Sven is planning to write.'

Charles Winthrop looked out of place as each member of the select audience shook his hand and congratulated him on his writing. A beautiful young girl of about eighteen years, gushed, 'Oh, Mr Drummond, your books are so inspiring, I always insist on reading a chapter before retiring, I keep your signed copy under my pillow,' she added, shyly.'

A security man tapped Mr Winthrop on the shoulder and said, 'Mr Drummond, sir, there is a telephone call for you at the reception desk, I believe it is from your daughter, it seemed quite urgent.'

Mavis, he thought, I wonder what she may want, I thought she was still at university, she is not due home till the end of the month. 'Hello, is that you Mavis? asked Mr Winthrop. 'Yes dad I'm at the hospital, Oh, it's terrible dad, it's mam, she's taken an overdose of the pills she was prescribed, she's in a coma, you best come over as soon as possible.' 'Oh my God,' exclaimed Mr Winthrop, 'I'll be over right away' and dropping the phone, said to the receptionist, 'get me a taxi for the private hospital at Parkside, right away! he said eagerly.

The doctor looked up from his file and asked, 'Mr Winthrop?

'Yes,' he answered and asked, 'is she going to be alright? The doctor looked at Mr Winthrop, as if he had recognised him from somewhere and deciding against it, and said, 'she is still in a coma, I'm afraid, we have done all we can to help her, you may go in now, but only for a short while' and turning gave the file to the nurse added 'I shall be on call, so keep me up to date, during the night.' 'Yes, doctor, 'answered the nurse. Mr Winthrop sat down on one of the chairs next to the bed, his daughter Mavis, sitting opposite. 'Oh, what have I done,' he said out loud, to his wife, as she lay, eyes closed, slowly breathing, 'I've brought all of this down on you poor Beryl, haven't I? I should have taken your advice and left well alone this idea of writing books and now look of the state of things,' he cried.

'Oh Dad! and standing up, his daughter said, 'this has nothing to do with you, if the truth be known, you had a terrible life with mam, she never gave you credit for anything you achieved, always complaining, criticising every little thing you did. You have done everything for me, best schooling, always there for me whenever I needed you, what did my mam do?, bloody nothing, but complain,' she said and furthermore, 'you devoted your life to that Union as their secretary, collecting dues in all weathers, visiting sick employees, making sure their families had enough to get by on while they were on the sick and what did you get for it, most of them thought you were a bloody fool, to go out of your way to help them,' she added.

Mr Winthrop frowned and said, 'now, Mavis, I don't want you talking about your mother in that way, yes, we have had our differences, I agree, but she never caused me any real trouble' and added. 'As for the Union, it was part of my life, it was a part of me,' he emphasised. 'Well, I'm sorry dad, but I think you are a bloody fool, God's fool, more like it and He has got you entertaining the whole bloody world with your antics. You have everything a man could wish for now, money, respect, success, people look up to and admire you' and pausing, said 'and all you can think of is mam lying there on the bed, still having her own way with you, still trying to control you. 'Yes, I have thought of that and I know she was always threatening to leave you for some other man, I used to listen at your bedroom door when I was a little girl, I used to think, I wish she would go and leave us in peace, to lead a normal life without her,' she concluded.

Mr Winthrop lowered his head and whispered, 'I think you have said quite enough my girl, now go on, off you go and leave me with your mam.' Mavis sat back down and then stood up again and said, 'alright dad, I'll be going, it was only a coincidence that I happened to visit mam, when I did, it was a good job anyway that I had a last chance to see her.'

Mr Winthrop looked up from the bed and asked, 'what do you mean, last chance, she's not going to die is she?

Mavis looked down at her father and said, 'It doesn't look good dad, I can tell you, the doctor is waiting for the lab report, before deciding on what to do next,' she added.

Mr Winthrop, eyes downcast, uttered, 'I will stay with her for now, you go on home and wait for me, I will be along later.' Mavis just nodded and quietly closed the door behind her.

THE FINAL CHAPTER

Mr Winthrop was sat at his desk typing on his old typewriter. He slowly pressed each letter with one finger, click, clack and finally twisted the typewriter barrel to read what he had read.

He had left the telephone receiver off the cradle, which had never stopped ringing with recorded messages left from, Alistair Wainwright, Geralyn Holmes, and a multitude of people wishing to talk to him.

I do wish they would leave me in peace, he thought. He was still dressed in his black mourning clothes and shuddered at the publicity that surrounded the funeral. The reporters had stood at a respectable distance, during the ceremony, but rushed to the funeral car leaving the cemetery, trying to photograph a glimpse of Mr. Winthrop and his daughter.

The newspapers had wasted no time in bringing up the notion of an unhappy marriage with his diseased wife and an imaginary sordid affair aligning him with Geralyn Holmes.

Mr. Winthrop, head in his hands, wept,' I never meant all this to happen, it's all too much to bear, why Oh why couldn't I have been happy with life with Beryl before all of this happened? he cried.

He slowly opened the large drawer in his desk and uncoiled a long hessian rope. He stepped up the old wooden steps placed near his desk and standing on his desk, threw the rope over the low wooden beam.

Mr Winthrop was found the next day hanging above his desk. There was a message typed on his old typewriter, which read,

Dear God I am sorry that it has come to this and did not want this kind of fame. I did not realise the pressure it would put on me and my family and are therefore, removing myself from the situation and now realise, I should have been most careful of what I prayed for.

7

THAT SPURIOUS OBJECT OF DESIRE

LAST SUMMER'S HOLIDAY

He had been staying with her parents for the past two weeks, which now began to tell on him. Her father was genial enough, but her mother, he soon discovered, suffered terribly for her religious piety and seemed intent on passing it on to everyone. He had met the girl whilst on holiday last summer and was at a time in his life when he seemed to be at odds with everything. He had hoped that the holiday would give him the opportunity to relax and take stock of things.

They had met during the second week of his holiday. She was sat alone at a corner table in the hotel restaurant, at the time of day when it was busy. He had walked past her table intending to seat himself near the open doors leading out into the gardens, but an elderly couple appeared at the doorway and promptly sat down.

Without a second thought, turning he decided to approach the table where the girl sat. 'Excuse me,' he asked, 'is this place taken? The girl looked up, lowered her eyes and shook her head. He sat down and picked up the menu and decided on his order. Putting the menu aside he took a good look at the girl and noticed that she was remarkably beautiful with long auburn hair way past her shoulders. She had a swarthy complexion, which was accentuated by hazel green eyes.

'I was thinking of ordering the fish,' he said, addressing the young lady. 'Well I wouldn't, if I were you,' she said, looking up quickly, 'They had a bad case of food poisoning when I visited last year and had a terrible to do, about it. Try the roast beef, it's always a safe bet in this place, I always say,'

He immediately noticed a foreign accent mingled in her conversation, but could not place it. 'Yes, I'll try it' and hoping to make conversation, added, 'so you visit here every year, do you? he queried.

She looked at him, as if she was about to choose her words carefully and said, 'My parents have been visiting since they were first married and it has become a bit of a tradition now,' she replied.

'Oh, so your parents are here as well?' 'No, they left last Saturday; I am staying until the end of this week.' They both returned to their menus and spontaneously, the girl smiling asked, 'It is your first time here, isn't it? I saw you walking along the beach yesterday morning' and laughingly, added, 'you looked terribly alone and had such a pensive look on your face, I was about to ask you if you were alright when I saw you from the balcony.' 'Oh, did I? he answered, blushing slightly.' You are probably right, I seem to be at odds with myself lately and if I am honest was wishing for the weekend, so I could return home.'

'Yes, being alone in a place like this can be terribly boring, with no company, I was beginning to feel a bit like that myself,' she added.

Without hesitation he said, 'Well, why don't we go out somewhere nice, it would make a nice end to our holiday.'

The girl looked down and answered, 'I am not sure about that, as I have only just met you, but I could let you know sometime later.' 'Great,' he replied, 'let me give you my phone number and let me know.'

The waiter finally arrived and took their orders. When their meals arrived they politely exchanged small talk whilst eating and before parting, the man said, 'my name is Stanley.' She lowered her eyes and replied quietly, 'mine is, Loretta.'

He waited apprehensively for the rest of the day for a call from Loretta, but finally decided not to look for her and retired to bed early. The next day he had planned for a local tour of a Stately home and kept looking at his mobile in case she called. He arrived back at the hotel late and as the kitchen was closed he sat in the lounge eating a sandwich and drinking tea. He thought of Loretta and wondered where she was and considering he only had two days left of this holiday, thought that there would be slim chance of making any friends now.

'Stanley,' a voice said behind him and quickly turning, he saw Loretta standing near the lounge entrance door. 'Hi! he said, and smiling asked, 'How are you? 'I'm fine,' she replied. 'I had a few people to see before the end of the holiday and having got that out of the way I wondered if you would like to go out somewhere tomorrow?

'Why, yes, of course I would,' he replied and added, 'I visited a Stately home today and it was a terrible bore.' 'Don't worry about that,' she said, 'I know of a lovely place where I can take you and it is quite secluded' and laughingly, said, 'so we may be able to get some privacy from prying eyes.'

ON THE BEACH

He was sat on a large leather chair in the foyer of the hotel waiting for Loretta. They had arranged to meet at ten o'clock and the large clock on the entrance wall showed ten past ten.

She suddenly appeared coming down the long winding hotel stairs. She was all in white with a large sunhat propped to the side of her head, except for a bright yellow chiffon scarf around her neck. Stanley was quite taken aback and promptly stood up and waved to her. She smiled and acknowledged him.

'My goodness! Stanley cried, as she approached him, 'you look absolutely splendid.' 'Thanks,' she said, in an offhand way. She looked at his small shoulder bag and added, 'I hope you have brought your swimming trunks and beach towel.' ' Oh, I'm sorry, I didn't realise we were going to go swimming,' he said, apologetically.

'More sunbathing I was thinking of, but if you wish to take a chance on swimming in this sea, you are more than welcome to, as for me, I prefer, secluded sunbathing.' 'No, that will be fine with me, but I am afraid you will have to wait for me to go and get them from my room, I won't be long.'

He returned via the long hotel stairs and scanning the reception area caught sight of her sat on a large leather sofa, chatting with a man. He felt a sudden tug of jealousy, wondering who the man could be.

'Oh, you are here,' she said, looking up and standing up she turned to the man and said, 'Goodbye' and taking Stanley by the arm walked to the hotel entrance.

'Who was that? He asked her, 'I thought you may have introduced me,' in an attempt to hide his jealousy. 'Oh, just someone I met last year here at the hotel and ever since has not stopped pestering me.'

Stanley felt relieved and glad she was holding his arm in such an intimate way and said, 'Well why don't you tell him so and make done with it.' 'Oh, I don't know, he's harmless enough I suppose and anyway,' she said grinning; 'I guess I must just like his attention towards me.'

Stanley looked into her face, but could see no emotion and thought, 'What a strange girl.'

The sun was bright and the day warm, when they arrived at a secluded part of the beach. Loretta dropped her large beach bag on the sand, followed by her large sunhat and rolled out the beach mat.

Stanley unrolled his beach towel, placing it next to Loretta's. She kicked off her sandals and reaching for her large bathing towel, wrapping it around her, beckoned Stanley to hold it for her, while she shimmied out of her dress. Stanley appeared embarrassed and turned away as she stood into her bikini bottom, pulling it up. The towel slipped down revealing her bare breast. Stanley lowered his eyes and she grinned and picking up her top, slipped it under her towel.

'Thanks,' she said and smiling added, 'I never had you down for the shy type.' Stanley appeared flustered and wondered if she had purposely set out to entice him, but just smiled back and said bravely, 'I'm not really, you just caught me off guard, that's all.'

She draped her towel over her beach mat and then kneeled down and stretched herself across the mat. Stanley removed his trousers and shirt, revealing his bathing shorts and string vest.

'I see you've come prepared,' she said, jokingly and reaching into her beach bag produced a large tub of sun cream. She offered some to Stanley and commenced to smooth herself all over her body.

Stanley couldn't contain himself and uttered, 'You are very beautiful, you know' and with a passion added 'I should imagine lots of men have said that to you, though.'

She looked aside and said, 'Yes, lots of men have said that,' and added, 'I only wished they could see something deeper than that, something more meaningful.' 'Well, maybe you have not given them chance enough to get to know you,' he replied and added, 'I should like to get to know you better and I am sure we would have a lot to offer each other.'

'What a strange man, you are,' she said happily. 'I thought the same about you,' he replied. There was a brief pause and looking at each other, they both burst out laughing.

That seemed to break the ice and Loretta asked Stanley lots of questions about his background, did he have a girlfriend, was he ever married.

Stanley just shook his head and said, 'No, I guess I'm a pretty sad fellow really.' 'Oh, I'm quite sure that is not true, I really think you are a bit of a dark horse myself,' she said, slyly.

They spent the rest of the day chatting, until the sun was suddenly overshadowed by some clouds. 'I think it is time we started back,' said Loretta. When they arrived at the foyer, Stanley turned to Loretta and asked, 'Would you like to have dinner with me this evening, I am sure you could recommend a decent restaurant, seeing as you know this place so well.'

She paused for a moment and looking into his eyes, she said quietly, 'Oh, Stanley, that is a wonderful idea and I know just the place,' she said enthusiastically.

'Great! replied Stanley, 'I shall meet you in the foyer at eight o'clock.'

DINNER AT EIGHT AND THE DAY AFTER

They were seated in the dimly lit part of the restaurant. The crystal lights were reflected in the bulbous brandy glasses, drained after a sumptuous meal. Loretta leaned forward and whispered, 'This is a frightfully expensive restaurant Stanley, I do hope it doesn't make too large a hole in your pocket.' Stanley smiled and replied, 'This is my treat Loretta and money is no object, I have had a wonderful day being with you and hope you have too.'

Loretta smiled shyly and said, 'Yes, it has been nice, hasn't it, it is a pity we met so late into the holiday' and added 'I should have liked to have got to know you better.'

Stanley, quickly replied, 'Well it may be the end of the holiday, but it doesn't have to be the end of our friendship, does it? Loretta, paused and said, no, I suppose it doesn't only...'

The waiter approached the table and interrupting Loretta, enquired, in a clipped foreign accent, 'Is everything alright, monsieur? Stanley looking irritated by the interruption, said, 'yes, yes, it was very nice thank you' and added, 'could I have the bill please?

They arrived back at the hotel late and sitting in the empty lounge, decided to have a nightcap, before retiring. They waited quietly as the waiter brought the drinks and hoping to break the awkward silence, Stanley asked, 'What time is you flight, tomorrow? Loretta, looking sad, replied quietly, 'I get a taxi to the airport for around six o'clock.'

It went silent again and for what seemed an eternity, Stanley suddenly blurted, 'Look Loretta, let's not end it here, I feel awful, us having just met and maybe not going to see each other again, can't we just go out tomorrow morning, maybe go out on the lake?

Loretta looking close to tears, replied, 'Oh, Stanley, I would rather not, I think it best we end it here, it may make it worse drawing it out, I have had fun and would like you to respect my wishes and let us part now.'

Stanley looked Loretta in the eyes and was puzzled by her lack of emotion and said, 'Alright Loretta, if that's what you want' and standing up, added, 'Well I guess this is really goodbye then.' He walked towards the lounge doors and decided not to look back.

Stanley arrived back in his hotel room and slowly undressing, felt weary and saddened at the outcome of the evening. He wished he had never decided to come on holiday and wondered if it had at all been worth all the effort. He thought of Loretta and realised that maybe he was being just a bit too optimistic about forming a lasting relationship with her and the distance between them now seemed insurmountable.

It was well past two o'clock when Stanley finally got off to sleep.

The telephone jangled loudly, stirring Stanley awake and reaching for the phone, he sleepily said, 'Hello, who is it?

'Stanley, it's me,' gushed Loretta, breathlessly. 'Oh, hi,' replied Stanley, this is a lovely surprise and fell silent. He could hear Loretta's breathing on the phone and still waited. Finally Loretta said, 'Listen Stanley, I hope you don't mind but I just had to call you to say I am sorry about last night, I guess I was just tired,' she paused and added 'oh, I don't know what I'm saying, I just wanted to see you again that's all, would you still like to go out on the lake, like you suggested last night?

Stanley felt annoyed at this sudden change of heart and his better judgement told him to say, no, but then his feelings gave way and he replied, 'Oh yes, Loretta, that would be great.'

'See you in the foyer at about eleven then,' she said happily? 'Yes, see you then,' he replied.

They had chosen a small motor boat with Stanley at the helm and slowly chugged out to the middle of the lake. All the while, Stanley was thinking, Should I ask her, but fearful of the reply he may get. He looked at her sat at the rear of the small punt and marvelled at her beauty. The morning sun was warm on their faces and Stanley not being able to contain himself any longer, said, quietly, 'Listen Loretta, I think I have fallen in love with you and I want us to be together, I don't want this to end here.'

Loretta appeared shocked and replied, 'Oh no Stanley you mustn't, you must not talk that way' and pausing she added 'I tried to tell you last night, but was interrupted by the waiter, the reality of it is, I have already got a boyfriend and we are planning on getting married.'

Stanley looked surprised and replied, 'Oh no, I can't believe it, I felt sure you liked me, I was sure of it.' Loretta quickly replied, 'I do, I like you lot, but I just thought you wanted to be my friend, that's all and added 'look I have got a card for you, I was intending to give it to you this morning, but forgot' and passing it to him, he slowly opened it. It showed two little bears hugging and underneath read, 'Real friends are hard to find, but I have found one in you.' Underneath was signed, Always, Loretta with an x next to it.

'Oh that's nice, thank you,' said Stanley and added, 'but nevertheless, I am not giving up on you' and bravely said, 'I shall pursue you. This is not the end. Loretta, looked him straight in the face, but just wore a blank expression, revealing nothing. 'Anyway, continued Stanley, you could at least let me take you to the airport, and see you off.'

Loretta, seemed to force a smile and replied,'Yes, off course Stanley that would be lovely, I will meet you in the foyer at say six o'clock?

'Yes, I shall be waiting,' replied Stanley.

Stanley was sat in the foyer apprehensively waiting for Loretta and looking at the clock it showed six twenty five. He intended to enquire at the reception but was met with a queue, waiting for people to book in.

He went straight to the front and said, 'Excuse me, I am terribly sorry, but I was to supposed to meet a Miss Loretta... and forgetting her name, the receptionist replied, 'If you are referring to lady you were with this morning sir, I am afraid she checked out of the hotel this afternoon around, three o'clock."

Startled, Stanley asked, 'Did she leave a message for me? The receptionist appearing irritated, replied, 'I'm sorry sir, but you will have to excuse me as I am dealing with a customer and then added 'I believe she was to due to fly out at seven fifteen.' 'Thank you, thank you so much' and looking at the clock he said to himself there is still yet time. He ran down the steps of the hotel and hailed a taxi, shouting, 'To the airport, as fast as you can, I will make it worth your while.'

He paid the taxi driver generously and ran into the airport departure lounge, looking at each departure display. He finally reached the international departure display and at the bottom was flight MA 202, departed, seven twenty.

Stanley felt weary and tired and head bowed, slowly walked out of the airport and feeling devastated, hailed a taxi back to the hotel.

THE LETTER

The letter arrived two months after Stanley returned home after his holiday. He had thought of Loretta a great deal, but as the months passed he gradually got accustomed to not thinking about her every day.

He settled back down to working in his father's large publishing company, which took him abroad on several occasions. As an assistant chief executive he met several young women on his travels, but would always look for the qualities he saw in Loretta and would invariably return to his hotel disappointed. He confided his feelings with an associate publisher of his own age and was told, 'Well what do you expect? This feeling always persists with unrequited love.' That did not matter to Stanley, he still missed her.

So it came as quite a shock when receiving the letter which started with, Dear Stanley, Hi, how are you? I am fine and have been at the family farm these past six weeks. I'm sorry I could not let you see me to the airport, but I was feeling very confused and could not feel I could handle another goodbye. I got your name and address from the hotel, I had to persist, but they eventually gave it to me, I think it was because we have had a long relationship with them. She continued, I am writing to you to tell you that I told you a lie about having a boyfriend that day on the lake and there is no other way of saying it, but I was frightened about what my parents would think about what you said, you see my mother is very religious and would never let me marry outside our faith. Anyway, I told them all about you and how kind you were to me and they seemed to take a liking to you, even though they have never met you. My adopted brother suggested we invite you to our home for a holiday, my parents thought it a great idea, but I don't know how you feel about that. So please do let me know if you are willing to visit us, I do miss you a lot, I really do. She just signed it, Loretta x.

Stanley read the letter several times, each time hoping to read something that would tell him she had other ideas, other than friendship, but could not find anything, she seemed to be making overtures, but only indirectly. He eventually decided not to reply and was beginning to feel angry about the whole situation. He did however, feel a respite from the previous situation and felt confident that just maybe, she was actually trying to pursue him.

It was some five months after the holiday that Stanley received the phone call. 'Hello! came a faint, excited voice, 'hello is that you Stanley? 'Who is this?

asked Stanley. 'It's me,' came the faint voice, 'Loretta!
'Oh hello,' replied Stanley coldly, 'what do you want?'

'Did you receive my letter I wrote to you about three months ago? she enquired. 'Yes, I did,' said Stanley and fell silent.

The phone went quiet and for a while Stanley thought she had hung up and
then said, 'Hello, are you still there? 'Yes, said Loretta quietly, I just had to
phone and tell you that I miss you, I really do and my parents are asking about
you, are you coming to visit us?

In an offhand sort of way, Stanley said, 'listen it is a bad line, so write me your
address and telephone number and I will let you know' and hung up. Stanley
felt he had regained some currency in the relationship and now feeling stronger, felt certain that she was trying to pursue him.

THE HOLIDAY

Stanley looked down through the aeroplane window as it circled and commenced its approach to landing. They had flown over a pale green ocean,
passed over a large natural harbour and could see a large domed church on its
approach. Sun washed limestone houses from a village appeared below and
fields of red soil and finally the runway came into view as they touched down.
According to the flight attendant there had been considerable rains these past
weeks, which had left bright green succulents sprouting from the loose stone
walls that lined the fields.

The heat was stifling as the door opened and he stepped down from the plane
and squinted in the bright sunlight. He was glad to get to the air conditioning
of the airport arrivals. He was quickly through customs and walked through a
long glass panelled corridor, finally arriving at the barrier of airport arrivals.

There was a long thick rope looped across chrome poles with people holding
cards with names and companies written on them. He scanned the area looking for Loretta, but she was nowhere to be seen. Suddenly from behind him
someone called, 'Stanley?

Stanley turned and there stood a young man in shorts and sun hat. 'Are you
Stanley? Stanley nodded and the young man said, 'I thought so, Loretta gave
me a pretty good description of you, my name is Gaetano, I am Loretta's
brother. Unfortunately, Loretta could not make it to the airport, but I am sure

she will explain it to you and you will understand.'

Stanley felt a sinking feeling in his stomach and angry at the thought that she could not have at least made the effort to meet him at the airport.

It was now two weeks into the holiday and Stanley was sat on the balcony of Loretta's family summer villa, overlooking a pale green sea. On his arrival he discovered that Loretta had taken a job a week before with a tourist company on the other island. It meant that she was away most mornings leaving him with Loretta's mother.

Her mother would arise at four thirty, for mass at five fifteen. It would invariably wake him up and he would struggle to get back to sleep before the heat of the morning sun blazed through the light summer blinds.

He would later find her mother sat in the kitchen with her prayer book, head bowed, with hands clasped. 'Good morning Stanley, have you slept well? she enquired. 'Yes, very well,' lied Stanley. 'I have prepared some coffee and cheesecake for your breakfast,' she said. 'Oh, that's lovely, thank you very much.'

'Will you be seeing Loretta this afternoon? she enquired. 'Well I was hoping to, but I think she may be taking a group out on a private tour this morning and I am not sure when she will return.'

'You know,' her mother said, 'when she arrived back from holiday, she never stopped talking about you, about how you were so kind to her and the gentle way she treated her.'

'Really,' said Stanley, looking astonished, 'she certainly did not give me that impression,' he replied. 'Ah, but you don't know my Loretta, do you?, she said and added 'I think she is more fond of you than she cares to admit. My son and father will tell you the same, they were always asking, 'Who is this Stanley, she is always talking about?

Whilst musing this on the balcony and feeling more confident about the relationship, Loretta suddenly appeared in the doorway, wearing light blue summer shorts and open top and sitting next to him, asked, 'Are you enjoying yourself Stanley, do you like our beautiful islands?

'I should like it a lot better if I were to see more of you,' he replied. 'I am so sorry about that Stanley, but as I explained to you, it was a job I have been wanting to do for a long time and could not possibly turn it down. I love being with people and all the attention I get, but I do miss and think about you during the day and do look forward to seeing you on my return.'

Stanley saw this as a chance to broach a subject he had kept hidden for so long and looking Loretta in the eyes, he clasped both her hands and uttered,

'Oh, dear Loretta, you are so ravishingly beautiful, I am just so lost for words. I want you for my wife, want you to have my children. I am very well off you know, you need never work again. You could have everything money could buy and more, you would be getting a loving and devoted husband' and added 'listen Loretta, I am even prepared to live here with you and your family, and change my religion. In a year's time I shall inherit fifty one percent of my father's large publishing company.' Loretta, pulling her hands away with eyes staring replied.

'Oh Stanley, you are intent on spoiling this holiday aren't you, I thought I made it quite clear to you before, yes, I am fond of you, but I could never marry you, for a start you are much too old for me and quite honestly, I don't love you, for heaven's sake, don't you realise that by now!

THAT SPURIOUS OBJECT OF DESIRE

Loretta's brother came into the lounge where Loretta and her mother were sitting. 'Well, did he get off alright? asked her mother. 'Yes, yes, he did,' replied, Gaetanto and turning to Loretta, said, 'I do wish you would clear up your own mess in future and leave me out of your chaotic romantic affairs.' Turning to his mother he said, 'I am going to bed, I have an early start in the morning.'

They both watched television for a while and her mother stood up and turning the television off, sat down next to Loretta and said, 'You know my dear, that was a very dear man you went out of your way to hurt today and I think you have treated him quite shoddily and I am still not sure of your motives.'

Loretta flicking through a fashion magazine, looking up replied, 'Oh mother I don't expect you to understand, money is not everything, you know, or the fact that he said he loved me. This has happened to me many times before, but I know better, he is just another one of those men who think they love me, but it's not true. I am just an object of their desire, they only think they love me when all along they are just attracted to beauty, they are in love with beauty, not me.'

8

MOTHERCHILD

THE OLD MAN'S HOUSE

I had often seen the old man whenever I visited my friend at his home. She would often go to her grandfather's and keep him company for an afternoon. I would arrange to meet her there, so we could go on out afterwards for a meal or to see a play. The house was a mid-terraced two bed-roomed pre-war dwelling with an outside toilet at the end of a long narrow garden. A metal bath hung on a large nail outside the parlour door, leading out in to a small narrow yard; which ran along the side of the house. An old-fashioned, rusty tyre-less bicycle was propped up against the yard wall, standing between several old stone flowerpots full of grass. The garden was overgrown with weeds which sprouted through the ancient flags, leading to the toilet. Everything about the garden smelled of decay and of times long past. The inside of the house was little better. As you entered the narrow hallway, the faded wallpaper was worn shiny at the painted dado rail. Large tarnished gold-framed sepia pictures hung on old loose faded wallpaper. To the right, a door led to the front room, which I had never seen opened. At the end of the hallway there were two stone steps down to the parlour, which was lit by a small electric light bulb hanging from a long wire. In one corner was a large glass-fronted dresser, much too big for the parlour, dominating the room. On the dresser were china sets on each shelf and old porcelain vases with artificial flowers. Near the dresser, stood a small round black lacquered table. It held three silver framed photos. A large one in the middle with two small ones each side. In the large one was and old sepia photograph of a soldier in khaki uniform with a rifle stood to his right. Draped on the photo were three war medals with ribbons attached. In one of the two smaller sepia photographs were a group of soldiers in khaki uniforms stood to attention. The other showed soldiers on a steam ship with their packs slung over their backs, cheering and waving to the crowds on the quay below.

CONVERSATION IN THE PARLOUR

We were sitting with my friend's grandfather in the parlour on two large wooden framed chairs close to a large fireplace. Her grandfather sat on an upholstered high-backed chair, directly in front of a fire which burned brightly casting long shadows on the ceiling. The fire was stiflingly hot, for a summer's day. The coals hissed and spluttered giving off hot gases and smoke which was quickly sucked up the chimney.

Her grandfather was a small framed man with bright blue watery eyes and white wispy hair. He normally sat with his hands clasped together in his lap, and would turn his head and lean towards you when he was spoken to.

'I think we have backed up the fire with a bit too much slack today grand-dad,' said my friend. He nodded his head and gave a far away smile. 'It's much colder today, isn't it,' he replied. 'The dark nights are closing in, it will soon be winter.'

My friend turned to me and gave a knowing smile. 'It is still summer grand-dad,' she said. 'Don't you remember Mum took you to the seaside last week? He frowned and then a smile of recognition lit his face. 'Oh, yes, I remember now, I don't know what I could have been thinking of,' he said. He turned to me and said, 'I never used to be like this you know, it was the war that did it with my hearing, it was noise of those dammed bloody shells,' he said.

'Now granddad, you told me you didn't like talking about the war, now don't go upsetting yourself again.' He smiled at her and said, 'Your grand-mother, when she was alive, God bless her, once said to me, Alfred, you left me in 1914, a young man and came back an old one. She would try her best to cheer me up, always putting a hot dinner on the table, and talking to me as if I were her little boy. Now eat up Alfred, you've got to build up your strength and be happy again, like you were before you went off to war. You know she would spend hours in the garden, just for my sake, planting flowers and growing vegetables. She said, she wanted me to look out of the parlour window and see something beautiful and take my mind off the war. When my old soldier pals came to visit me, she would send us to the front room, out of her way. I don't think she liked hearing about the war, as you know, not many of us came back from it. I would often go to the memorial statue near the church and read out the names of the lads from my regiment who were killed. I don't think your grandmother ever really understood the lads, or myself, for that matter. We all started out thinking it was going to be a great adventure and we would return heroes before Christmas.'

MEMORIES OF AN OLD MAN

I had arranged to meet my friend at her grandfather's house, early evening and then go on to see a play. I had arrived early and knocked on the door and waited some minutes and began to wonder if anyone was at home. After a while, I heard a scraping of a key in the lock. Her grandfather slowly opened the front door and said, 'She's not here yet, but come in and wait for her.' He led me down the hallway into the parlour. The fire was out and the room felt damp and cold.

'Shall I light the fire for you? I asked, 'it's quite cold in here.' He leaned back in to the upholstered chair, seemed to struggle to catch his breath and nodded his head. I lit the fire and I pulled down the fire hood to draw it. The room was slowly getting dark and I asked the old man should I put on the light. 'The bulbs gone and I don't have a new one,' he said.

I sat down close to the round black lacquered table and picked up the small, silver framed photograph of the soldier's waving from the steam ship. 'Are you in the photograph,' I asked. The light from the fire lit up both our faces and cast shadows on the walls and ceiling. 'Yes,' he said 'I'm the soldier with my arm around my pal.' He was called Tommy Bradshaw, we started work together at mill when we were both fourteen. He was a great lad, always joking and having a laugh, you couldn't wish for a better pal than him,' he said.

I could see he wanted to talk and leaned forward in my chair and listened. 'I can still remember it, as if it were yesterday. We both signed up on same day, did our training at local barracks and shipped out together. We arrived on a Wednesday, on Tommy's seventeenth birthday. We spent weeks marching for miles in the rain and freezing cold. We kept hoping that something would happen, we couldn't stand the monotony any longer. Then one bright November day, we were given orders that we were going up to the front in the morning.' The old man paused and wiped a trembling hand, across his mouth, continued, 'It took five days to march and meet up with our regiment. Our first job was to go out at night and lay barbed wire in the dark. Nothing much happened, except the occasional flare and a rumble of gun fire, now and then. It was very exciting for us and we would always return back at our dugout, exhilarated, feeling like heroes.'

'One night I was shaken out of my sleep by the sergeant and he whispered, come on lad, we are going over the top this morning. It was just before dawn and we all stood in a line, rifles in hand, waiting for the order. The sergeant stood with one leg propped against the ladder, waiting for the lieutenant's whistle.'

BOMBARDMENT

'The lieutenant looked at his watch, blew his whistle and climbed to the top of the ladder, waving his pistol in the air and shouted, 'come on lads, let's go! Several flares went up, lighting up the sky, I scrambled up the ladder, out on to a large open field, dotted with bomb craters and rolled barbed wired and started running in the direction of the flares. Tommy Bradshaw was close behind me, I could hear him panting and shouting to me to keep your bloody head down. I was terrified! I just kept on running in a mad panic, expecting to be killed at any moment, bullets were flying left and right of me and one caught my right shoulder and spun me around, hurling my rifle out of my hand. I felt an awful burning pain, before falling in the mud and that's what probably saved my life, because in the next instance there was a barrage of shells exploding in front of us. Somebody shouted, 'Bombardment!

A shell landed within five feet of Tommy Bradshaw and hurled him in the air and he landed, twenty feet behind me. I could just about make him out, he was lying across barbed wire, still clutching his rifle. It was a terrible thing seeing him lying there, staring with, blood flowing from his mouth. Tommy then tried to lift himself up and gave a cry out and fell back.'

The old man then did something quite out of character. He leaned forward and stretched out his hands and put them on my shoulders. His hands were trembling and putting his face close to mine, said, 'I loved that man, like he was my own brother and to watch him die like that, it was horrible.'

He continued, 'I could see a smouldering bomb crater to the left of me and I painfully, crawled towards it and slithered down its side. I must have passed out for some time, because when I came too, it was raining heavily. My left leg was bent under me and my right leg was under water. I could still hear distant shelling and gunfire and I must have passed out again, because when I woke up, I could hear men shouting and calling for help. I then tried to crawl up out of the bomb crater and after several attempts I reached the top. It was just getting dawn and it was very strange, because it was a beautiful dawn, but all around me there were dead bodies of men that I knew and soldiered with. It was horrible! He put his hands to his face and then started to shake and sob uncontrollably. Just then the parlour door opened.

MOTHERCHILD

I turned around and saw my friend standing at the top parlour step, holding a small box. She looked at me and said, 'I'm sorry I'm late, I had to go and get an electric light bulb for the parlour.' Turning to the old man, she said, 'What on earth is the matter granddad. Why on earth are you crying and upsetting yourself? I was still holding the small silver framed picture in my hand and turning to me she asked, 'Has he been talking about the war again?

I must have had a guilty look on my face, because the old man quickly looked up at her and said, 'It's not his fault, it's something I have wanted to tell somebody for a long time.' He turned to me and wiping his mouth said, 'Anyway, I managed to stand up and stagger towards our trenches, stepping over dead and dying men, crying and calling for help.'

'Granddad, my friend interrupted, 'you could not have helped them, they were young boys dying, calling for their wives and children and their comrades.'

He turned to my friend and said, 'Is that what you think? is that what you think? He repeated. 'My pals were terrified of dying, yes, we all were, but they were not calling for their brothers, sisters or friends, yes, they were crying and sobbing like little children, but they were not calling for their wives or comrades.

They were sobbing and crying for their mothers. I still can still hear it in my head to this day, I shall never forget it for as long as I live, Mama! Mama!, they cried help me please Mother! I don't want to die, Mama, Help me!

9

A SAD AFFAIR

AT THE SUPERMARKET

Kurt had returned to Southern Africa from Europe in late February and was now sharing a small house with a doctor friend from the local Bush hospital. The hospital was one of those built before independence during the time when the country was a Protectorate and was then called, Bechuanaland. The staff were mainly expatriates, except the nurses who were usually locals. He had been invited on several occasions to give what the Registrar called In house lectures to the doctors and nurses. His topics ranged from educational, agricultural and health problems, which he was able to impart some of his knowledge, as a researcher in Anthropology.

The university had just finished its summer break and most of his days were spent idling under a Jacaranda tree sat outside the entrance to the house, reading and listening to his Deutsche Gramophone, of the complete works of Schubert's Lieder.

Other times were spent shopping at the local Spar which was situated in the Mall in the centre of the village. There were all kinds of hardware, millinery and vegetable stalls surrounding the supermarket and he was often looked upon as a kind of oddity to the locals who would follow him with their eyes as he passed by each shop and then each aisle of the store. By the time he had arrived at the checkout he felt as if he had been given a thorough going over with the staff and would invariably invoke sniggers from the checkout girls when he addressed them in his clumsy attempts at the local language.

On one occasion one of the checkout girls who he recognised from other visits gave him his change and receipt and seemed to be whispering something which was quite inaudible with the general noise. He decided to ignore it but was held back from behind by the checkout girl opposite. She said loudly, 'she wants to go out with you and has written her cell number on your receipt if you want to give her a call.' She then nodded to the girl and gave a squeal of laughter and turned back to serving a big blousy lady who gave him a grin which lit up her moon-like face.

He suddenly felt all his nerve leaving him and quickly made his exit to the store, still clutching his change and receipt which the security-man had great difficulty trying to pry out of his hand to check the contents of his shopping.

This was quite common in all of the local shops where there must have been a lot of pilfering going on. He had always viewed the lack of commodities and money with the locals as a kind of acceptable consequence of a comparatively new and developing country with such a small population. They never seemed to complain, at least not openly and carried a quiet dignity which could both unnerve and disarm one.

He stopped a taxi further down the Mall and arrived back at the small house just after his doctor friend had arrived and related the story of the checkout girl. 'I would be very careful of getting involved with the local women,' he said and added, 'they carry lots of other diseases, besides the obvious ones, you know.'

Kurt retired to his bedroom and sitting on the edge of his bed, dipped his hand deep down inside his pocket, revealing small change with the supermarket receipt wrapped around it.

He carefully unravelled the receipt and on the back was written, 'my name is Neo and my cell number is, 07576204631, call me.' He thought of his doctor friend's advice and decided against it.

THE PHONE CALL

The summer rains followed and time passed slowly. He grew tired of listening to his Schubert's Lieder and would spend ages throughout the day looking through his kitchen window, watching people, heads down, hurrying in the torrential rain. He had given several talks at the local hospital, but they had not revealed any new friendships.

He grew restless and tried to re-read some of his research papers, in the hope of presenting at the university in the capital. He knew what the real problem was; he pined for female company, not necessarily sexual, but just someone to talk to and thought of the supermarket girl, Neo.

Oh, she probably has forgotten all about that a long time ago, he thought.

Never the less, he searched his wallet, but could not find the supermarket receipt. Ah well, maybe it is just as well, considering the advice his doctor friend had told him, he thought.

Finally, the rain had stopped and he decided to go out for a walk and on passing his bedroom mirror, there stuck to it was, the supermarket receipt, 'Yes! he cried and called the number on his cell phone.

The cell phone seemed to ring for a long time and Kurt was about to give up when a quiet voice enquired, 'Who is it? Kurt, cleared his throat and replied, 'I'm the guy you spoke to at the supermarket a while ago and you gave me your cell number to call you, do you remember? The phone went silent what seemed an age and then she replied, 'Oh yesss, drawing out the word, I remember you now' and fell silent, This annoyed Kurt and finally asked, 'well what did you have in mind, are you still interested? wishing he had never phoned in the first place.

'Oh, I am sorry,' she replied, 'I did not mean to be rude, it is just that I never thought you would call me, that's all, I'm glad that you did, though,' she said happily.

'What time do you finish at the supermarket? he asked, regaining his composure. 'Oh, usually around eight o' clock,' she answered. 'Right, I will be outside waiting for you then, see you around eight, Ok? 'Yes, she said, that will be great, see you then.'

All day long Kurt thought about the evening and meeting the girl. He tried to remember what she looked like and recalled she had long braided hair, with the light complexion of the Khoisan, although he was quite sure she was from the Bamanguatu, having included the San in his thesis, which he would soon be submitting to the department of Anthropology at Guttenberg University.

African women had always attracted him and he felt an affinity which he could not place. Maybe I have some far distant African relative from my past, he thought, although these feelings were always somewhat exterior to his normal feelings about himself and his earlier lifestyle in Germany before arriving in southern Africa was totally different.

The evenings were still warm, so he dressed in a light blue shirt and yellow trousers. He carried a small white canvas bag over his shoulder, for his phone, wallet and sunglasses.

He arrived at the Mall at around seven. The bright market lights bathed the walkways and the shops, giving an appearance of daylight, with the black diamond canopy sky above. He strolled around looking in the different shops and reached the supermarket entrance at quarter to eight and stood on the hardware store steps opposite.

A very emaciated thin man in torn trousers and jacket with a lapel ripped approached him and with his face close to him, blurted in a drunken manner, 'I'm waiting for my girlfriend, she works at the supermarket.' Kurt instinctively stepped back and stepped down two steps away from him. The drunkard stepped down one step towards Kurt and said threateningly, 'I know you, I saw you talking to my girlfriend in the supermarket, well let me tell you rra, she belongs to me, see! Kurt angrily replied, 'Let me tell you Mr, I do not think I would be interested in your bloody girlfriend, whoever she may be, now get going, before I call the police,' he shouted. 'Police! Shouted the drunkard, 'my uncle is the police sergeant of this village and I could get you into big trouble, I can tell you!

A small crowd of people gathered around the two men. One big women stood in front of Kurt with her arms outstretched and said to the drunken man, 'Rra! Go! Go away please and leave this kind man alone, Monna!

Kurt felt weak, but grateful to the big woman and felt a tug on his arm and turning around, there stood the supermarket girl. 'Come! Come! She said softly, 'let's go!

'Neo! Neo! Cried the drunkard, 'it's me, your boyfriend! The big woman squealed with laughter and shouted, 'Haaay! Monna has taken Neo for his girlfriend,' she cried. The whole crowd started to jeer and laugh and pushing the drunken man further away from Kurt and Neo, disappeared in the crowd.

'Phew! What was that all about? Asked Kurt. 'Oh it's nothing really,' said the girl. 'He's always around the supermarket bothering the young women, he gets it in his head he owns you if you just talk to him.'

'But he knew your name, you must have said something to encourage him,' replied Kurt. Neo smiled and said, 'You don't know African men, do you.'

They had walked away from the brightly lit Mall and turning to Neo, Kurt asked, 'Where would you like to go then? I was thinking we could go to Tindi Lodge for a meal.' 'Oh, I have to go home and bathe first, if we are going out,' she answered. 'Is it far, because I can phone a taxi,' suggested Kurt. 'No, it's just a short walk through those trees and bushes,' replied Neo.

A LIGHT IN THE HUT

They walked along the road in the dark for a while and then Neo, taking him by the hand, whispered, 'come, this way' and stepped over a small wall down into a walkway between two large bushes. Kurt squinted in the dark and said, 'I can't see a thing, it's so dark.' Neo laughed and replied, 'don't worry I can walk this way with my eyes closed.'

They walked on, brushing past bushes and sometimes getting light from a waning moon. They rustled through some bushes and finally came to a clearing with several huts dotted around it. A small light from one of the huts lit the area in front of it. 'There, that's where I live,' said Neo, 'come on.'

They reached a dark green wooden door with old clay pots around it and succulents sprouting out of them. Neo stooped down and pushed a small pot to the side and produced and old long silver key and placing it in the key-hole, gave the door a shove with her shoulder. 'It's a bit hard to open when it's been raining,' she explained. She stepped up the one step leading into the hut and Kurt followed behind her and noticed an immediate odour of candlewax and cooked food.

The light he had first noticed was a candle placed on a metal plate sat on a small window ledge, next to the door. He glanced around and saw a large bed centre to the room, with two large pillows in pink pillowcases. Each side of the bed, were two metal boxes and wooden crates, used as furniture. There was a table in the corner with metal plates and cutlery and several candles stacked on one of the plates. Beneath the table were two black tripod pots for cooking.

What impressed Kurt was the cleanliness. All of the bedding was washed and placed at the bottom of the bed. Hanging on rails were freshly washed women's underwear and stockings. The stone floor had been scrubbed and waxed to a shine. The corner opposite the table had a small curtain, which covered a small vestibule. Next to the bed was a large metal bath, which Neo proceeded to drag across the room close to the candlelight. She then lifted a large plastic water container and slowly poured the water into the bath, the water giving off a translucent light against the shadows. Without warning she commenced to disrobe, unbuttoning her supermarket uniform, dropping it onto the floor. She crossed her hands over her shoulders and pulled her lace undergarment over her head, throwing it onto the bed.

She stood completely naked and stepped into the metal bath and bending over, proceeded to wash her arms and shoulders with a bar of washing soap. Kurt instinctively turned away and Neo seeing this laughed and said, 'You appear to be ashamed to look on a woman's naked body, what strange people you Europeans are.'

Kurt turned and looked down and said, 'It's not that at all, it is just not normal for us to see a woman disrobe in front of a complete stranger.' 'Then you must be either afraid or ashamed to let people see you as God intended,' she said 'It is just considered undignified for a woman to let a man see her naked that's all,' he replied.

She stood out of the bath and picked up a large bath towel from the bottom of the bed and wrapping it around her body, said, 'Ok, if that's what you think about it, it's alright with me' and added, 'I just wonder what intentions you had when you phoned me, that's all.'

Kurt could feel himself getting upset with the way this relationship was going and had to admit, this girl had a quality of honesty he had never experienced and decided to tell her just that. After he had finished, Neo beamed and said, 'do you know, I do not even know your name, but already feel very close to you.' Kurt felt an unusual closeness and a feeling of meaningful warmth and compassion for this young girl and replied, 'My name is Kurt.'

Neo finished dressing and Kurt dragged the metal bath to the door and emptied the water down a grid. 'Turn it over and place it near the bed, for it to dry.' said, Neo.

Kurt lifted the metal bath and slipped on the wet floor dropping the bath with a resounding clang on the stone floor.

'Eish! Exclaimed Neo,' that gave me a bit of a scare.' 'I hope I haven't woken anyone up in the yard, as it is getting late now,' said Kurt. 'Don't worry,' said Neo, most of the people will be still be drinking at the Shabeens, they won't be back till late, but I will have to wait here till my sister comes, so I can give her some money.' Kurt was about to ask the reason for this added delay, when there came the sound of a young child whimpering.

Neo looked at Kurt and smiled and walked across to the vestibule and drew the curtain. There stood a little girl naked, holding an old piece of blanket around her.

Kurt looked at Neo in astonishment and said, 'You never mentioned you had a child.' Neo looked puzzled and asked, 'does it make any difference to you that I do?

'Well no, it doesn't it has just come as a surprise to me, that's all,' he replied and asked 'where's her father? Neo ignored the remark and walked over to the child and picking her up said, 'There now little one, did we wake you up? And carrying her over to the bed, laid her down pulling the blankets close around her. 'I'm hungry mummy,' said the little child. 'Didn't your aunty give you something to eat? she asked the little girl. 'No,' replied the child, she just came and lit the candle when it was getting dark and left.'

She sat on the edge of the bed and beckoned Kurt over to her, to sit down and said, 'My sister should have been here by now, and so I don't know what to do.'

'It doesn't matter,' said Kurt, 'I'll go to the Mall and get some food for us, and I'll be right back.' Neo, shook her head and said, 'no you better not, it's too dangerous for you to be going back that way on your own, I'll go.'

Kurt, dipping his hand in his shoulder bag produced his wallet and giving Neo some money said, 'Go to Chicken Licking, they should still be open now and bring some food and drinks for all of us.'

Neo gave Kurt the silver key and said, 'lock up, after me; I will give three knocks on my return.'

Kurt lit several candles around the room and sat on the edge of the bed next to the child and said, 'your mummy is going to get you something to eat, she won't be long. I am going to stay and look after you.'

The little girl gave Kurt a shy smile and covered her head with the blanket. Kurt smiled back and asked, 'What is your name? 'Boitumelo,' answered the girl and covered her head again.

Kurt felt a sudden weariness in both body and mind and lay across the bed. He wondered how he managed to get himself mixed up with this young woman and now this small child and felt he had been drawn unintentionally into something quite out of the ordinary. He could see that he had always been an observer, watching them go about their daily lives, but now he felt he was experiencing life in a different dimension, having once observed, but now participating, as if on a different plain.

The sparsity of everything saddened him, but he began to feel at one with everything, as though he belonged and saw himself no different and much like the child and Neo.

He laid across the bed and closing his eyes, must have fallen lightly asleep, because he was suddenly aroused to a tapping on the door.

'Kurt! Called Neo, 'it's me, open the door! Kurt jumped up and on opening the door, Neo rushed past him and said, 'you had me worried for a moment, I thought you had left and taken the key with you.' Kurt mumbled, 'I couldn't have done that.'

Neo threw a raffia mat on the floor and placing candles around it, laid out the food. 'Come,' she said, 'let's eat.'

They sat on the mat and Neo held a metal bowl under Kurt's hands and poured water over them. Kurt obediently washed his hands and she gave him a small cloth to dry them.

The little girl sat crossed legged between them and ate hungrily of the chicken and chips.'

'Are you going to stay with us tonight? Asked Neo, 'I think it would be better. It doesn't look like my sister is coming now and I can't leave the girl alone again.' Kurt nodded and said, 'I'll call my housemate and tell him.'

They finally lay on the bed with little Boitumelo laying between them. He woke up once during the night to find the little girl's arm stretched over his neck, holding him tight.

When he finally woke up the animals were stirring outside and Neo was lying close to him, with her arm wrapped around his waist. He gently moved her arm and quietly sat up and could see the little girl sat on the stone floor, playing with a rag doll in the dawning light.

He quietly opened the door and slipped silently out of the hut and arrived back at his house early and found a note left by his doctor friend to call his professor at the university.

It was some days later that he received the phone call. 'Kurt, it's Neo,' she said. 'Oh Hi,' said Kurt, 'I was meaning to phone you but I have had to go to the university in the capital to see my professor, I got back late last night.'

'I was wondering,' said Neo, 'if you could give me some money for gas, till I get paid at month end? 'Yes, of course I can Neo, shall I bring it to the Mall tonight.' 'Yes, that would be great,' replied Neo and added 'You know I was disappointed to find you gone in the morning when you stayed last week,' she said in a quiet voice. 'I still haven't made you my own yet, have I? she laughed. 'That will come,' said Kurt, 'I am sure of it, aren't you? he asked. 'I do hope so,' she replied.

A SAD AFFAIR

He was waiting outside the supermarket till well past eight and wondered where Neo could be. The staff were turning off the lights and closing the doors, when Kurt asked the security man, 'Have you seen Neo, the cashier? I was supposed to meet her here at eight.'

The security man thought for a while and answered, 'oh, yes, that Neo, well I didn't see her turn up for work today, in fact I am sure she didn't, because her sister was looking for her.'He tried calling her on her cell phone, but kept getting an unobtainable tone. He decided to retrace his steps to the hut, but found it impossible to find it. He also thought of what Neo had warned him about the dangers of being in that area at night and finally decided to get a taxi home.

He arrived home late and tried calling her again, but the phone must have been switched off and wondered what could have happened to her.

He returned to the hut early the next day and found a group of people standing outside. One of the cashiers recognised him and called into the hut. He walked quickly up to the hut calling 'Neo! Neo! It's Kurt!'

To his surprise an older woman stepped out of the hut and asked, 'Are you Kurt?' Yes, yes, where's Neo? what's happened to her? he asked.

'I'm her sister,' she replied and she has had to go far away. She caught the early bus this morning and won't be coming back.' 'But I don't understand, didn't she leave a note? he asked.

'She told me she will try and contact you soon and not to worry,' she replied. 'But what made her go away so suddenly? he asked.

'She asked me not to tell you, but I think you deserve to know. Her husband is a violent man and she has suffered terrible abuse from him in the past, he found her at her auntie's house in another village and confronting her, asked, 'where's my daughter? and Neo told him, 'where you left her and he attacked her with a kitchen knife and nearly killed her, she came here two years ago and he found out that she was here in the village and was coming looking for her. The police have been informed, but they will do little as his family have relatives in the police force,' she added.

Kurt was sat on his bed when his doctor friend returned from the hospital and decided to tell him the whole story. The doctor listened quietly and finally said, 'Ah, Kurt, but you have been taken under the wing of Mother Africa and she has smiled on you, but her smile can sometimes bring sadness.'

Kurt is still waiting for that phone call that will tell him to come, so that the three may be together again, but the rains have passed and the winter is settling in with cold winds blowing in from the north.

10

PERCHANCE TO DREAM

THE CONVERSATION

'But at least you will have peace of mind afterwards, if you go' said the man's wife. They had had this conversation many times before, and it invariably ended the same way. The man would give a shrug, and say, 'Oh well, let's talk about it some other time, not now, I have to' and then make some excuse to change the subject. These conversations always had a weakening effect on his wife who had patiently laboured long on her husband's recurring problem. His work had always taken him away from home for long periods, sometimes to foreign countries. He was an only child and his parents had devoted themselves to giving him the best education, money could buy. He now suffered bouts of anxiety and terrible feelings of guilt and shame, which impacted on his work and was beginning to be noticed by the Board of Directors in the large multi-national company he worked for. His bosses had thought he was overworked by the heavy schedules his work demanded and recommended he take a short vacation which would give him respite from the stress of his daily routines. His wife thought it an ideal opportunity to seek help with his recurring problem.

'What you want me to do is see a psychiatrist isn't it,' he said. 'There is nothing wrong with me, that a psychiatrist would be able to solve,' he added. 'But at least you would have peace of mind,' his wife stopped and realised they were going over the same subject without any progress. He looked into his wife's eyes and could see her despair and how it always left her upset, knowing she could do nothing to help him. He did want help, he knew that inwardly, but there was always a wall of resistance that prevented him from talking about it.

'Listen,' the husband said, feeling a need to reassure her, 'let's talk about it tomorrow morning and then decide what we should do about it.' His wife's eyes lit up with relief and added, 'yes, yes let's do that darling. I am so glad that you have decided to take steps to seekhelp.'

'I am not promising anything,' he added. 'Yes, yes, dear I shan't mention it again until you are ready to do so.'

He decided to retire early that evening and left his wife to browse a holiday catalogue and look for possible short breaks for them to consider.

THE DREAM

His wife was leafing through the holiday catalogue near a large open fire, thinking of the last conversation they had and was feeling somewhat re-assured that they may be making progress with the husbands problem. If only he could admit to himself, that he needed help, she thought, and was considering phoning the psychiatrist the following morning, to see if an ap-pointment could be made, when she was suddenly brought back to herself with a resounding shout, followed by a loud scream from upstairs. She froze, dropped the catalogue and ran to their bedroom, where her husband was sat upright in bed, hands clutching his head; his face wore an expression of abject fear. She moved quickly to his side, softly whispering, 'there, there dear it's alright; you've been having one of your bad dreams again.'

'Oh! My God,' he sobbed,' it was the telephone thing again, will it never end, I can't bear it any longer. I dreamed again we were sitting up in bed and the phone rang next to the bed, I answered it and my mother was on the line, asking me what time we were going see them for dinner on Sunday, I could clearly hear my father's voice in the background asking her to tell me to bring his favourite bottle of stout, for him,' he trembled and added, 'listen, I'll do anything to get rid of this misery, just do what you have to and let's sort this out before I go completely mad.' 'Yes, yes, dear! I will phone the doctor first thing tomorrow morning.'

'Doctor Fitzgerald? the wife enquired. 'Yes, doctor Fitzgerald speaking, came a soft voice, in reply. 'It's Miriam, Miriam Smith, doctor. We spoke a while ago, regarding my husband and I wondered, if there is the possibility of an appointment for my husband, at your earliest convenience, that is,' she added. 'You will recall, that in our last conversation, Mrs Smith, that if your husband is not willing to get honest with himself there is little or nothing that I could do to help him.'

'Yes, yes, I know that doctor, but I think he is now willing to at least recognise that he has a problem and wants help. His recurring dream, has become considerably worse and has asked me to contact you.'

'Well, that, at least may be considered a way forward in his coming to terms with his anxiety and guilt. I shall speak to my personal secretary and arrange an appointment as soon as possible. It may be wise to strike while the iron is still hot and while he is still in this present state of mind.'

'Oh! that is wonderful doctor, I am so grateful for all your help in these matters.' She was about to about to enquire about the possible time and day for the appointment, when the phone clicked and the receiver went dead.

IN THE PSYCHIATRIST'S ROOMS

The receptionist smiled, pressed the buzzer and said, 'Mr Smith is here for his three o'clock appointment, doctor Fitzgerald.' A low voice, hardly audible said, 'show him to my room nurse.'

The receptionist raised her head and said, 'this way, the doctor will see you now.' She led the way through a polished mahogany door, down a long corridor, with large gold gilt framed pictures of famous doctors hung on the dark maroon William Morris wallpaper walls. Their footfall was softened by the opulent carpet. On reaching the psychiatrist's door, she lowered her head forward and gently knocked on the door. Presently, the door opened and a large lady wearing a full length fur coat, turned sideways, nodded and slipped between the nurse and the patient, whilst waving a farewell to the psychiatrists inside the room.

'Mr. Smith,' the nurse said, 'for his three o'clock appointment doctor Fitzgerald.'

'Ah! Yes, Mr. Smith, do come in.' The doctor, tilted his head forward touched his short grey beard in a gesture of welcome, stood aside to let the patient pass him into the room. The room was spacious and adorned with heavy furniture. An open fire burned brightly in a large grate, above it on a large white marble mantelpiece stood a bust of a noted psychiatrist. Directly across from his desk was a padded leather couch. There were two large bat-winged chairs each side of the fireplace. 'Do come and sit down Mr. Smith, I feel our first appointment should be quite informal, a sort of getting to know each other, so to speak.' The nurse, silently left, closing the door behind them.

'Well now, Mr Smith, let us see if we can make a little progress today,' he said. 'I have an inkling of what the problem is from your wife, but would prefer to, hear it directly from you, straight from the horse's mouth, so to speak,' he said, grinning.

The man had a worried look on his face and stuttered, 'Well, I don't really know where to begin or for that matter, when it all started,' he said. 'It has seemed to plague me this past twenty years. The recurring dream which I have, always feels so natural and normal, I am lying in bed with my wife and the telephone rings, I pick it up and I can hear my mother,' Mr Smith pauses and swallows hard and continues, 'she is asking me to come to dinner on Sunday and she always asks me not to forget to bring my father his favourite bottle of stout.'

The psychiatrist looked at him, reassuringly and said, 'I think maybe the best place to start, would be from the very beginning, tell me a little about your childhood,' he asked gently.

'Well a lot of my time as a child was spent with my uncle Albert, who was a sailor who had retired early from the sea, due to ill health,' he said. 'Uncle Albert was my dad's brother and would take me to museums and sometimes to the cinema. My mother and father were always very busy with the business and uncle Albert always had plenty of time spare, so they thought it an ideal situation.' he added.

'So there were quite long periods of separation from your parents? the psychiatrist enquired. 'I suppose you could say that on looking back in hindsight,' the man said. 'I just never looked at it in that way before. In fact I now realise that my summer holidays were always spent with uncle Albert and most Easter times were spent at Blackpool, with him.' The psychiatrist paused and looking away into the fire he enquired, 'How was your relationship with your uncle Albert like? 'What on earth do you mean,' asked the man.'

'Only, that it would not surprise me to learn that you may have unconsciously created a father figure, in your uncle Albert, that's all,' he explained. 'Maybe I did, but what has that got to do with my fits of anxiety and panic attacks? he asked.

'You have not mentioned your unaccountable feelings of guilt and shame that your wife mentioned, when we first we spoke.' he added.

'Oh! Well! That! he said, 'I never considered that had anything to do with my problem, do you think my long periods away from my parents could have any direct effect on my current situation? he asked.

'Mr Smith,' the psychiatrist replied, I am simply pursuing all avenues and possibilities, that may have had a bearing on you current situation, you must try and understand that a young child's mind is very impressionable and estranged situations at early childhood could certainly create developmental problems.'

'Developmental problems? Doctor Fitzgerald! said the man,. 'May I remind you sir, that I carry the responsibility of Assistant Chief Executive at a multinational company with a gross annual earnings of over two billion Euros.'

The psychiatrist smiled unaffected by the man's sudden outburst of emotion and looking sternly at the man said, 'Mr Smith, it is not your adult lifes capabilities that is in question here, but rather the experiences of your childhood, the underlying influences that may have occurred and had a direct impact on your adult life,' he added 'there are subtle emotions, below the level of consciousness at work in childhood that require the utmost care and consideration when revisiting them under a controlled environment, one has to be most careful that one does not bring about more mental or emotional, if you prefer, problems on the patient.'

Mr Smith, went directly on to the defensive and replied, 'I am so sorry doctor Fitzgerald, as you can see, this is a very difficult and emotional time for me and has taken all my strength and courage to seek help.'

'Of course, Mr Smith, Of course, I do understand, perfectly, but if we are going to make any meaningful progress, we have to get to the roots and causes of the problem, which will require a great deal of honesty on your part, do you see? he added.

The man slowly nodded his head and replied, 'I shall do everything in my power to assist you doctor Fitzgerald, I feel I am more than halfway there already, in agreeing to come to see you.'

'Yes! That was an important step, but only the beginning of an inner journey for you Mr Smith,' he said. 'You see,' he continued, 'it is like as if our lives are large baskets with lots of different shapes inside. There at round, square, diamond and oblong shapes cut out of the basket, now there are also solid shapes of the same size and life has a nasty habit of shaking up these different objects until they each finally find there corresponding shape and drop through their respective holes, then we may find the answer to a lot of our emotional difficulties and make peace with ourselves,' he added.

'Well it all sounds very technical, but I think I understand and grasp what you mean,' replied the man.

'Good, very good,' said the psychiatrist, 'now I am going to prescribe a little something for you, to help you deal with some of your anxiety, I want you to take one of these tablets twice a day, until further notice. On your way out, my secretary will make another appointment for you, I was thinking of in two weeks or so?

'Yes, that will work out quite nicely as my wife and I are planning a little trip next week abroad.' 'Wonderful, Mr Smith, the rest is bound to help and prepare you for your next appointment.' he added.

THE DOCTOR'S OPINION

Doctor Fitzgerald was stood with his back to the fireplace, and said to his associate sitting in one of the bat-winged chairs, 'yes, an unusual case of sorts,' he said, 'the poor chap is quite at odds with himself, so I thought maybe a little parlay with you may help Tom.'

'From your conversation and the information you gleaned from his wife, I would say, he is avoiding certain issues in his past. I wonder if the shame and guilt you mentioned, is indirectly as a result of his time apart from his parents and an underlying, unconscious resentment towards them, which is now manifesting itself as episodes of guilt and shame, now they are both been dead for twenty years. His sudden emotional outburst when you raised the question of developmental problems, possibly touched a nerve there.'

'Yes, I am inclined to agree with you, I was thinking of putting him under hypnosis and regress him back to his childhood, what do you think, Tom? asked doctor Fitzgerald.

'Yes, I seem to remember reading somewhere in one of our scientific journals of a case where a patient had been subject to hypnotherapy and had induced false memories under regression based hypnosis,' replied the associate. 'I am not sure that may help, but it is certainly worth noting Tom,' said doctor Fitzgerald. 'I have prescribed him diazepam twice a day to address his anxiety, but as we both know that is only dealing with the symptoms, not the problem. I shall start him on a course of mild hallucinogen's to open him up and then proceed with the regression based hypnosis,' added doctor Fitzgerald.

'Yes, that may be a way forward,' replied Tom, 'I should have also added that one has to be most careful with this form of therapy and medication, as there have been rare cases of permanent regressive episode.' 'I shall bear that in mind Tom, but I am most grateful for this little parlay, it has given me plenty to think about before his next appointment which is next week.'

ON THE PSYCHIATRIST'S COUCH

'Are you quite comfortable, Mr. Smith? asked Doctor Fitzgeral. The man was lying on the psychiatrist's couch, with doctor Fitzgerald sat on a stool close to him. 'Yes, I think so,' replied the man.

'Now you must try and completely relax and clear your mind of every little problem that may have been bothering you and listen to my voice,' said Doctor Fitzgerald softly. The potion I gave you earlier will help you to see things a lot clearer,' added the doctor.

'Mr. Smith,' continued the doctor. 'I want you to close your eyes and imagine, emphasising the word and repeating, imagine a time way back in your childhood, way back as far as you can remember,' he said. 'I am not sure when that would be,' answered Mr Smith. 'It does not matter, just try to recall an incident, say with your father or mother, when you were very young,' said the doctor reassuringly.

Mr Smith thought for a moment and then as if his voice was coming from somewhere in the distance, said, 'I seem to remember when I was three or four, being in the parlour at the back of a shop my parents were getting ready to open, they must have just started out in business, my mother was opening a large wooden crate and taking out vases and decorated plates, ready to be put up on display in the large bay window of the shop.'

'Can you tell me what you were feeling at the time, Mr. Smith, was there anything of importance that occurred? asked the doctor softly. 'I seem to remember a feeling of being alone, even though my mother was sitting next to me,' he replied. 'I remember sneaking out into the dark hallway and hiding in a cupboard, next to the cellar door. I waited for a while, thinking my mother would come and find me and be glad to see me,' he added. Then without warning started to cry like a little boy, 'I waited and waited, but she never came,' he said, weeping, 'I was so frightened, that I must have fallen asleep, because when I woke up, I was in my bedroom and it was dark.'

'And what do you feel now about the incident? asked the doctor. 'I am not sure, maybe I still feel as if I had been neglected,' he answered. 'Does that make you feel angry, or resentful towards your mother? asked the doctor

'Oh! No I am quite sure of that,' replied the man. 'Are you quite certain Mr. Smith? It is very important that you be perfectly honest with yourself for us to make any progress, I shall require your rigorous honesty.' The man lay quiet for a while and his slow breathing became more pronounced until he finally exclaimed and burst out loudly, 'No it's not true! he shouted. 'I hated her! I hated her! Then as if awakening, he added. 'No I don't mean that, I mean, Oh I don't know what I mean,' he sobbed.

'That is quite alright Mr. Smith, quite alright,' repeated the psychiatrist, 'just a little upset from your past, you are doing very well, I can assure you, 'he added.

'Do you think so, really,' asked Mr. Smith. 'It seems I have hidden a lot of my feelings and emotion from my past and I cannot for the life of me, understand why,' added the man. 'The reasons why, is of the least importance Mr. Smith. The important thing is that you have confronted them and see them in their true light, which is a great breakthrough, I can assure you,' added the psychiatrist.

'Yes, I feel much better already, having got that out,' said the man, 'but it is quite a shock to realise that I have hidden such feelings about my mother for so long,' he added.

The Psychiatrist smiled benevolently and said, 'Mr. Smith, you are on the most important journey of your life, your journey to self-awareness, which will give you release from all your past experiences and like we previously discussed, you will drop nicely through the basket and finally make peace with yourself,' he said reassuringly. He continued, 'Now I want you to once again relax and clear your mind completely and tell me in your own time where you are now.'

The man's features became composed and his lower lip began to slowly tremble, as if he was trying to say something but it would not come out. 'Relax,' said the psychiatrist, drawing out the word 'and tell me, where are you now Mr. Smith?

The man's lip stopped trembling and said quietly, 'I am with my uncle Albert at the seaside and we are coming down the steps of the bed and breakfast hotel where we used to stay. It is very busy at this time of the year and there are a lot of Scotsman, wearing Tam o'shanters, arm in arm with their girlfriends. We are now walking along the promenade and there are many people pushing and shoving to get to the front of the pier,' he added.

The man then fell silent and after a few minutes the psychiatrist asked, 'and what happened then?

The man's face took on a look of anguish and surprise and repiled. 'He let go of my hand, he let go of my hand! he shouted. 'I was lost and frightened and I kept calling, Uncle Albert, Uncle Albert, where are you? where are you? and then I cried for my mum and dad, but they never came,' he sobbed.

PERCHANCE TO DREAM

The couple are both sat near the large open fire, Mrs Smith, calmly leafing through a holiday brochure, while her husband is reading his newspaper. 'It was so good of your company giving you extra time off for another holiday Alfred,' she said joyfully.

'Yes, I am looking forward to it,' he replied. 'You know dear that doctor Fitzgerald is a marvellous man, he has done such wonderful things for me, you know, allowing me to come to turns with my past which I had so cleverly hidden. I feel like I have been given a new lease of life, a brand new start,' he added.

'I am so proud and happy for you my dear and you look and sound so different,' replied Mrs Smith and added 'and that new medication he has prescribed for you certainly seems to be working, you have not had a dream episode or anxiety these past six weeks.'

Mr. Smith stretched his arms, yawned, looking at his watch, said, 'Good heavens, is it that late? I think I will go to bed. Don't be late will you dear, we have to finish packing tomorrow. I will go and check I locked the front door,'

'Alright dear, I shan't be long,' replied his wife. He stood up, stretched again and disappeared into the hallway. She could hear his soft footfall on the carpet and just then the phone rang and his wife heard him answer it and spoke to someone in a quiet voice. The phone clicked and his wife enquired, 'Who was that dear?

'Oh! It was only mum and dad reminding us to come over to dinner on Sunday, he said happily and then added, 'I must remember to get father his favourite bottle of stout.'

THE STRANGE CASE OF
PROFESSOR KOESTLE

VOICES IN THE HEAD

'It is always much better, to get your thoughts down on paper before they have chance to formulate into something unlike the original, before they have chance to allow the voices in your head change what you really wanted to write,' he said. I smiled, gave him a nod, as if it was understood that voices in the head could be so irritating, and turned back to the text book I was reading. He pensively, looked down at his notebook, scribbled a note, looking around, before slipping it into his coat pocket. He was was no stranger to the university library, although no one appeared to know of him. For myself, I often saw him tucked away in a corner; head bowed busily writing in his notebook. This had been the first time he chanced to speak to me, although I had noticed him previously looking in my direction, when looking up from my reading. He had an intense air about him, which gave one the impression that he was in a constant state of anxiety. His face was pale and washed with weariness, but with bright intelligent eyes, which appeared to be constantly deep in thought.

The next time I saw him was a few weeks later in the first week of term, when most people were occupied with courses and registration. He was stood in the libary, near the renewal desk, holding a large leather attaché case. He was quite short, which I had not noticed before and although he carried a fragile countenance, his stature was quite robust. He was occupied with one of the library clerks, and commenced to place the case on the desk, and proceeded to take out several books. The clerk was checking the books into the library system, when he suddenly turned to me as I passed by the desk. He looked frightened and my first instinct was benevolent, and was about to utter something, when he moved close to me clutching my arm, looking at me with his eager intelligent eyes, said, 'Please, you have to help me!

I made an instinctive attempt to move away from his clutching hand, but he held firm, while forcing a small notepad into my hand. Within a moment he had released his grip on my arm, grabbed the attaché case from the desk and made a start for the revolving doors towards the entrance of the library.

I turned to the desk clerk, who gave me a look of bewilderment, shrugged her shoulders, and buzzed for the next waiting student. I stood transfixed for what seemed an age, still holding the notepad in my hand, and decided to proceed to the quiet room I had booked earlier that week.

On arrival at the room, I placed the notepad on the table, next to my reading notes, which I was preparing for a future conference. I then did something quite out of character, which was to close the door quietly, while sliding the bolt to secure the door. I suddenly felt certain unease about the notepad, but then smiled at the thought that this poor fellow was having such an unnerving influence on my senses.

I sat down at the table, and commenced re-reading some of the main points of my address to the conference and after scanning a few pages, my curiosity getting the better of me regarding the note-pad, I succumbed and flicked through the pages at random.

The notes appeared to be in the nature of some linguistic fieldwork on some obscure African language. I say this with some knowledge of this mode of fieldwork, having spent several years in Southern Africa researching endangered languages. I wondered if the poor fellow had been aware of my past research and had singled me out for his interest in me and the unusual encounter in the library.

It was only when I closed the notebook, that I noticed some writing at the top of the cover. Adjusting my glasses, I could see a telephone number, next to a scribbled address. Below it was written, They're back, the voices are back, please get in touch with me as soon as possible, I am desperate.

THE PROFESSOR

I decided to give it some consideration, before I should call him and made several discrete enquiries about him. The story I got was that he used to be a Doctor of African languages at the university many years ago, but left to take up a Professorship at a Southern African university. The last news that we heard from his university was that he had been there for a semester and then commenced some fieldwork with an informant from some remote village, miles from any civilisation.

After several months he turned up again wandering about a cattle-post belonging to the Dean of the Faculty of African Languages. He was in a terrible state and talked gibberish for hours repeating the same sentences in some strange language, over and over again. The Dean nursed him for several days until he began to come around and recognise his surroundings.

He was then transferred to the local hospital for observation. He spent several months at the hospital and slowly recovered from the ordeal. The chief psychiatrist saw him regularly and after several weeks decided to refer him back to the UK, for further observations. Before the Professor left for the UK he contacted the university, sending them a corpus of his research, hoping some students would take up some of the linguistic fieldwork he had done.

He returned home some months later and had contacted his home university. They were quite pleasant about it and received him in for a visit, but explained that they could not offer him any posts at present. He did accept their kind offer, as he put it, of allowing him free access to the facilities of the university library.

I picked up his notebook and made a note of his telephone number and on arriving back at my office, I decided, with some trepidation, to phone him. The phone rang for some time and I thought, maybe it was not such a good idea to get involved.

I was about to happily put the phone down when a soft voice whispered, 'Hello? 'Is that Professor Koestler,' I enquired. 'Yes,' came the reply. 'who is it? I gave him my name and he said, 'Oh! Thank you so much for phoning me, I have been hoping you would call.'

I waited for him to speak and after a long delay, he said, 'I am sure you will find this most peculiar, but I wondered if we could possibly meet sometime, maybe at my home?

'If you could explain to me why I should visit your home, when we have not even met, except for the encounter in the library last week,' I answered. 'Yes! Quite,' he said. 'As I said it may sound awfully strange me, singling you out like this, but I would rather not discuss it over the phone. If I could possibly beg your indulgence, as one colleague to another, I should be most gratified,' he said.

My first reaction was to find some excuse and decline the offer, but he seemed a totally different person to the one I had met in the library. Even his voice sounded different. There was none of the intensity in it. I paused before deciding and I could hear his gentle breathing, waiting for my reply. 'What is your address? I enquired.

MEETING AT HIS HOME

I pulled up on the opposite side of the street, to where he lived. The curtains were drawn closed and there were dustbins overflowing with rubbish in the overgrown front garden. I may have been mistaken but I felt certain that I thought I saw the front room curtain open slightly and then pulled back quickly. I walked quickly to his front door and rang the bell. There was a light showing through a small gap in the front room curtain window which convinced me that he must at home and had looked out when my car had pulled up across the road from his house. I tried to peer through the torn dirty net curtains hanging on the front door, when suddenly the door swung open.

I was startled and instinctively stepped back. He stood in his dressing gown, holding a large book to his side and whispered, 'Oh! Thank you so much for coming' and invited me in.

The hallway was dimly lit and there was a damp musty spell to it. It was over furnished and I had to sidestep a large oak dresser and a tall hat stand. I followed him down the hallway and entered the front room to the left of the stairs. It was a large brightly lit room with a round oak table in the middle. All along the walls were book shelves to the ceiling. Two high backed chairs stood each side of an open fire grate, where a fire burned brightly. He waved me to one of the seats and asked, 'would you like a drink, a cup of tea or something? I said, 'no thank you' and placed my attaché case, near the chair.

He sat opposite me and looking down at his clasped hands, he said, 'I cannot take too much reality, you know; not since returning from Africa. I have to indulge in books and research to get away from them.' His vagueness puzzled me and I had the feeling he was experiencing different levels of reality. I said gently, 'who or what are them?

He said, 'That I cannot answer, but feel something or someone has been trying to communicate with me. I have been away a long time you know and I do not really know where to begin.'

'Maybe that is the problem,' I suggested,' 'you could start from the time you left our university and took up the professorship in southern Africa'. 'Ah!

he said,' in a friendly way. 'I can see you have been doing your homework.'

I said nothing and waited for him to continue. He waited for a while and then said, 'When I arrived at the new university, I was given several leads which may have helped me in my research, but I am afraid they all drew a blank. Anyway, I settled down to the routine of weekly lectures and seminars and set up a team of students carrying out fieldwork. It was mainly routine stuff and did not give me much satisfaction.

Then one day I was called to the Dean's office and was introduced to a very thin old man who had lived most of his life in the central desert of the country. His name was Setalie. He told me that he was quite willing to assist me as a guide, informant and interpreter for the fieldwork I was doing. I was quite surprised that when he spoke, it was without the slightest accent. In fact his lips hardly moved when he spoke, but I could hear quite clearly every word he said.

I may hardly tell you that I was immensely impressed and invited him to the university staff refectory. He insisted that we sit away from the staff and I found a quiet corner where we could have some privacy. Setalie looked around him to see if anyone was in earshot. 'It is quite alright,' I said, 'no one can hear our conversation from here.'

He cocked his head to one side, as if he was listening in to the staff in the refectory, closed his eyes, opened them, smiled and said, 'I can hear peoples conversations from quite a distance.' He pointed and said, 'the young woman over there is arranging to meet the gentlemen sat next to her, to her house for ten o'clock this evening.'

The gentleman in question was a colleague of mine, the young woman a student, he had a reputation for being a womaniser, so it did not come as a surprise to me.

'Why, that is quite remarkable,' I said, 'how on earth do you do it? I don't know, I have been told by my tribesman that it is a gift, although some of the more superstitious ones think it is Taboo.' We talked for some time and he agreed to take me to a settlement in the central desert, where I could carry out my fieldwork. I explained, that it may take some time, because I would have to get government and university clearance and that may take several weeks.

He smiled and said, 'I believe you will find the people there, and their language very interesting from a linguistic point of view.'

I consulted with the Dean and applied for a fieldwork permit. During my fieldwork lecture I invited two of my doctoral students who were engaged in similar research. They seemed reluctant to discuss and made excuses about accompanying me on the fieldwork trip. I asked other students and one fellow said, that when he was a small boy his grandfather, on dark nights, would tell stories around their fire at the cattle-post of a mystical tribe who possessed strange powers, who lived on the central reservation in the desert. It was told that people who had wandered into the desert had disappeared without trace and on returning would lose their ability to speak and would eventually go mad and die in a state of apoplexy.

I dismissed these stories as mythical legends born of fear of the unknown. We departed for the central desert about a month later.'

IN THE SETTLEMENT

'On meeting Setalie's family, I settled down to collecting data from the selected tribe's informants, using Setalie as an interpreter. Slowly I began to understand the informant's language and recorded and documented sound samples of their speech, transliterating it into the International Phonetic Alphabet.

Then as time passed, to my surprise and bewilderment, I noticed that their lips slowly stopped moving and I was able to communicate with them without talking.

Whilst asleep I started to hear voices explaining to me of Setalie's tribe long ago, who were not of this world and had travelled many eons to earth and had settled in the remote part of the central reservation. As the dream progressed I could see that they were using some mystical force, which enabled them to abandon the normal form of discourse and start to communicate, using telepathic powers.

I woke up startled and terrified and wondered if I had been dreaming. I recalled the conversation and warnings of my students, when asking them to accompany me on my fieldwork. I lay for a while trying to compose myself and decide the best recourse for me to adopt to deal with these strange, but magical people.

I didn't have to wait long, because I was sure that they had been reading my mind and my intentions, when I heard the lock on my door click locked. I softly walked towards the door and could faintly hear someone standing outside and tried the door, which was locked, proving my worst fears.

I lay back on the bed and closed my eyes, wishing I had taken heed of the student's warnings, when very quietly as if from a distance a soft voice whispered to me, saying,

It is alright professor Koestler, you do not have to be afraid of us, we do not mean to do you any harm, but we we want you to help us.

What do you want of me? I asked and the soft voice replied, we want you to take our special gift and spread it throughout the world, so we may assimilate ourselves into other tribes, much like we have done with you,' he answered.

But how am I to achieve this? I am only one man, I couldn't possibly influence the rest of the world, you think to highly of me, I replied.

You must document our language and allow others access to it, it will not take long for them to be under our control, much like you are, he said, finally.

I thought, I must be still be dreaming, this cannot be possibly happening to me, but then the door slowly opened and their stood Setalie.'

'I must have passed out because I suddenly found myself alone and stumbling down a footpath. My shoulder bags were crossed around my shoulders and I struggled to stand upright. I sat down and took stock of my surroundings. I opened one of my shoulder bags and found neatly wrapped in leaves some dried meat and rice. There was also a large water container. My other shoulder bag contained all of my research work, with added suggestions in footnotes which must have been placed there for my attention. I must have wandered around aimlessly for a few days and finally arrived at a cattle post.'

I had looked at the professor the whole time he was talking and could see he was deeply distressed about the whole affair and would clasp his hands together as he related the events to me. 'Yes,' I said, 'I know pretty much what happened after that from your old university. I must say though, I do find it a bit alarming to hear what transpired in regards to your visit to that remote tribe,' I added.

The professor looked at me with an unnerving stare and said, 'I know it must sound incredibly bizarre to you, my dear friend, but I assure you, I sometimes have difficulty believing it myself, in fact I was convinced that it had all been a bad nightmare and I had been hallucinating, brought on by my isolation whilst in the dessert. It was only when I returned home to my house and settled down to reviewing my research that it started up again. It was insidious and started with what at first appeared to be whispering and I would catch myself pleading with them to leave me alone, I really felt I was going insane.'

'Yes, I know,' I replied, 'you always seemed preoccupied with something.' 'It was some weeks after my return from Africa, that I was woken up one night, in a cold sweat, having been convinced that Setalie was trying to communicate with me again.'

'Have you decided what to do, now you have related the story to me? I queried. 'I must admit,' he replied, 'I feel so much better having got it off my chest. It has been an immense struggle carrying this burden alone,' he answered and added, 'could we meet up again soon?

I left the professor with a promise to visit him again the following week and on arrival outside his house I noticed the heavy curtains had been drawn and there was no reply. I called his land line but got an unobtainable tone, the same when I called his mobile. I decided to leave matters alone until I heard from him again and still could not grasp the reality of the story he had told me.

THE PACKAGE

It was some six months later that I received the package. It was from the southern African university. I opened it and read a letter from the Dean of the Faculty, who informed me that professor Koestler had returned to the university and taken up his post again and had commenced lecturing on the fieldwork language he had been documenting. He had covered a lot of the corpus and had presented papers on the subject at several universities in South Africa, namely, Pretoria, KwaZulu-Natal and Witwatersrand. The professor had given the Dean instructions to mail a copy of his findings to me. He then went on to say that the professor had disappeared again and was thought to have returned to the remote village for further fieldwork research.

According to Setalie, the professor's informant, they had not seen or heard from him since his sudden departure from the village without any explanation.

I thought of the story the professor had conveyed to me and decided it was the raving of an eccentric old man. Never the less my curiosity got the better of me and after a few weeks I read through his transliterations and listened to some of his sound samples. It did not take me long to realise that the language was in no way out of the ordinary. In fact, it had certain words and phrases similar to the three Eastern Khoe languages I had documented for my thesis.

I decided to write a letter to the southern African university requesting permission to write up a paper on the transcript for submission to an up and coming conference on Typology and Endangered languages.

I presently received the authority to proceed with the paper I was writing plus an invitation to visit the university as a visiting scholar. Included with the letter of authority was a Grant of a Research Permit to do fieldwork. I though this rather odd, considering I was only requesting copyright authority, but what surprised me most was at the bottom of the letter, it was signed, best wishes, Setalie.

I decided to write a letter back to the university thanking them for their kind offer, but due to my workload this semester I graciously declined the invitation.

The rest of the semester was taken up with lectures and two conferences where I had the opportunity to present a paper and had not given any further thought to Professor Koestler.'

WHISPERS IN THE DARK

And so the strange case of Professor Koestler draws to a close with our storyteller sat with his wife on a cold, dark, winter evening. The wind howls, rustling the bare branches of the trees in the front garden. They are both sat close to the fire blazing in the fire grate, the flames casting dark shadows around the walls. They are warm and comfortable in two large leather armchairs, listening to a symphony on the radio.

'It's a dreadful night,' retorted his wife, 'it hasn't stopped raining since this afternoon and weather forecast says, it's not going to let up until at least next Monday.'

'Yes, it's pretty grim,' he said and added, 'the long range forecast has predicted a lengthy spell of wet weather with freezing ice to follow. It looks as if a few conferences may be put back due to two cancelled keynote speakers, although it could be a god send with the workload I have had this last year.' he added.

'Well, it looks as though it has all been worth it and turned out quite well for you now with your Associate professorship offer from the university, since you published that last paper on endangered languages,' his wife, replied.

'Yes, that came as quite a surprise,' he said and added, 'you know the faculty were going to...' 'and stopped in mid-sentence and cried, 'what was that?

'What dear? His wife replied,.

'That, that as if someone is whispering, can't you hear it? He asked.

'I can't hear anything,' his wife replied, 'it's probably the wind and rain' and laughing added. 'Gosh dear! you look as though you've seen a ghost! The storyteller ignored her remark and just stared into the fire.

'Hello! Came the whisper, it's me Professor Koestler, now I do not want you to be afraid of us and we certainly do not mean to do you any harm, but we want you to help us... '

ODYSSEY

OUT OF THE GARDEN

A large yellow butterfly hovered for a moment above Hindra's head, before encircling his naked body and flew up to a small thorny bush, settled and watched the still sleeping figure. The grass felt damp and warm, when Hindra awoke from his short sleep. He now felt relaxed and at peace with himself and the Garden. He sat up and saw his family, still near the water's edge. His mother and sisters were sat together, while his father and brothers played under the squat tree near where the stream met, and flowed over the small waterfall down into the main river flow. Hindra was not in the habit of thinking deeply, but now he began to feel a new emotion, which puzzled him. It was as if something was awakening in him, a new and wonderful feeling of freedom, which he neither knew nor wanted before.

What troubled him most was that although it was such a wonderful feeling, it somehow made him feel guilty that he should possess it. This made him frown at the thought of sharing it with any of his brothers, and especially not his sisters or parents. The feeling grew more intense and made him want to run and laugh wildly, but then as it subsided, made him catch his breath to stop it as if it should be suppressed. Suddenly Hindra struck on the thought of calling on the Garden to help, but felt an even deeper shame and quickly pushed the idea far back in his mind. But I will have to say something to the Garden, when we speak together at sunset he thought. Hindra had always been on good terms with the Garden and felt a certain pride when he thought of his obedience and love of the Garden, and how the Garden had loved him unconditionally. But now he felt lonely and troubled by these new feelings that seemed to be surging in and through him.

Hindra suddenly looked up and noticed his family had left the river bank, had walked way past the waterfall, and were now some distant past the meadow and into the thicket near the woodland.

He suddenly felt terribly alone, and shouted to them to wait for him, while breaking into a run across the meadow. It was now quite late in the afternoon, and dark clouds had gathered over the woodland and were now rolling and distant thunder broke out across the valley below. Gusts of wind were blowing the dry leaves near the water's edge.

Hindra was now running wildly towards the forest, intent on shelter from the oncoming storm. Rain started to fall in big drops and then great sheets whilst the wind blew, bending the branches on the tall trees at the entrance to the woodland. When he arrived at the thicket his family had disappeared into the forest, which by this time had become dark and foreboding. He was now panting heavily, out of breath and paused to rest and then plunged recklessly into the dark forest in the hope of catching up with them. He ran for some time while the last vestiges of daylight still pierced the dark gloom of the forest, but finally came to an abrupt stop when his head collided with a large branch stretching across his path.

He must have passed out for some time, because when he came too, the forest was pitch black and he was shivering violently from the cold. It was raining heavily and the sky was suddenly lit by bright flashes of lightening, followed by crashing sounds of thunder. He tried to get his bearing with each flash of lightening, turning once this way and then that way, looking for some familiar tree or bush to guide him through the forest.

All at once there was a blinding flash of lightening and almost immediately a resounding clap of thunder, which shook the earth beneath his feet, throwing him to the ground. A tree close by burst into flames showering great sparks into the black night sky, setting alight bushes partly dry from the forest covering. He drew himself to his knees, still dazed from the clap of thunder, and fell forward into a run, away from the now growing forest fire. He was soon near to exhaustion and felt he had been running for a long time. He could still see the fire a distant behind him, which was now lighting up the night sky, and made him soon realise that he had once passed an old dead tree some time before.

Close to despair, he kneeled down, head bent sobbing uncontrollably he cried out, 'Oh Garden,! dear Garden! please forgive me, it was not my intention to wander from you, nor have strange thoughts, which you would not approve of. Take me back dear Garden, never again will I stray from your clear and gentle path. Tell me clearly what to do, and I will do it without delay. please, please Oh Garden, Oh Mother help me please!

He was now frantic with grief, but stopped abruptly, hoping for a reply. The forest was now ablaze and crackling with the sound of burning, smoke spiralling in great plumes above the heat of the fire. He tried to listen, waiting for a thought or feeling that the Garden would soon come to his rescue, but nothing could be heard except his own panting breath above the roar of the burning forest. He finally stood up, his body blackened with dirt, covered with cuts and scratches from the flight within the forest, wiped his hands on his thighs, and stumbled away from the blaze. The night sky was ink black except for the rising moon, which was now glinting a ghost-like light through the silhouetted black trees. He stumbled on until the moon was high in the heavens, and could see in the distance a silver stream translucent with the light of the moon. Soon he could hear the bubbling sounds of the stream, and began to quicken his pace. He soon realised that he had been running away from the garden and had unwittingly found himself far south and to the east of the garden. The stream was sparkling with the reflection of the moon, and several rivulets had appeared, more numerous with the heavy rain. He crouched down in the shallow part of the stream putting his palms into the icy water, trying to wash the dirt from his trembling body. He shivered violently, rubbing his palms across his chest and stooping to rub some life into his cold frame. He stood erect stamping his bare feet in an effort to keep warm from the cold, and realising the wind had changed and was now drawing with it the heat from the burning forest. The desire to sleep wrapped itself around him, but resisted the temptation. He followed the stream in the hope of finding a landmark from which to take a measure of his place in the forest. He fell forward into a staggered run along side the moonlit stream, stopping only to take a breath. His eyes had long time become accustomed to the dark light of the forest, which now began to take on a deep red glow, lighting up the heavens.

Exhausted from his flight through the forest he slowed his pace to a stumbled walk, finally stopping to rest against a fallen tree. He had realised for some time that he was a long distance from his families resting place and had ventured far east of the garden into some unknown woodland. The moon was now high in the heavens, leaving a faint shadow on the forest floor. It was now quite black where Hindra stood, which instinctively reminded him of the darkness before dawn. Having felt some respite from the rest, he stumbled on following the faint light of the stream. The fire in the forest appeared to have subdued behind him and he shivered from the cold rain still falling heavy on the forest floor. Eventually, there appeared the faint, grey-leaden light of dawn, slowly changing to a lighter hue, which urged Hindra on, until unexpectedly he was out of the forest, onto a huge desolate plain.

He looked around him in the dawning grey light and could see a large hillock where there appeared to be a plateau in the far distance. The rain-leaden clouds had now become lighter with a fine mist soaking the bare rocks, which jutted through the dark earth of the plain. Hindra drank deep from the small stream, before turning his back to the forest and set out towards the plateau. A light fresh wind blew up from the east clearing the clouds; the sun's light burnishing the dawn sky. He walked on until he reached the foot of the hillock, which was now far higher than he first realised. The sun had risen, the warm air drying the wet rocks around him, filling the air with a pungent aroma.

Hindra decided to rest before attempting the hill, and looking back towards the forest he could see that he had been gradually rising above the woodland. In the distance, smoke was ascending from the burnt out part of the forest, the heavy rains having extinguished the burning trees. He started his climb when the sun was at its highest, bending low to avoid the heat of the day. He was now weak and hungry from the ordeal, but pushed on until he finally reached the plateau some time later.

He could now see in the distance the whole of the forest below him, the silver stream winding its way and bending out of sight of the plain. But the garden had disappeared from view. Instead there appeared to be a deep chasm beyond the forest and the snow-capped mountains high above the valley. Weary from the long climb and the flight in the forest, he laid down on a flat rock, the sun warm on his face. Sleep gently took hold of him and he slept a fitful troubled sleep.

He awoke with a start, but refreshed from the sleep. Surveying the small trees and bushes that were dotted around the plateau, he arose and walked towards a shaded part. There he found some wild berries, with a sweet, bitter taste and some red-skinned fruits. He ate hungrily, whilst wiping the juices from his mouth with the back of his hand. Somehow, he felt quite different to the way he was before he had slept. The powerful emotions that dominated him when he had awoken in the Garden had returned, but with greater intensity. But they now no longer troubled him; in fact he took a delight in feeling them. They gave him a kind of confidence he had never experienced before, which thrilled and gave him a feeling of strength. There was no longer present the feeling of guilt and shame, but one of pleasure, which made him feel he was at the beginning of new and exciting experiences. He no longer thought about, nor tried to communicate with the Garden and imagined how wonderful his life could now be to live alone and free with these new feelings. His past was something to be put away, to be forgotten. He no longer needed anyone, except himself and the new life within him.

Hindra spent some time looking around the plateau, before deciding to travel further east. After resting for a sunset, he awoke just as the sun was rising, ate some berries and headed for a small stream in the far distance.

By the time he arrived at the stream the morning sun was high and warm on his face. The stream had become quite deep in parts, through the heavy rains. He waded into the middle, the current gently swaying him as he tried to secure a firm foothold on the pebbled bed of the stream. The waters ran deep and he had to struggle to keep his head above the cold water. Seeing a large log coursing down the stream he grabbed hold of a large branch jutting out from the trunk. Holding on with one arm he waded further across the stream until finally he was close to the far shore. He stumbled up the pebbled river bed and collapsed on the sand, where he rested.

He travelled for a further sunset until he reached a small wood thick with young trees and bushes. Pushing his way through the woodland he could hear the faint sound of water. Suddenly, he was clear of the wood and far in the distance there was a sea inlet where large waves crashed on the long sandy causeway and in the mist could see a land far across the inlet, where on the shore a large fire lit up the surrounding area. Straining his eyes he could see people running along the shoreline.

He waded out into to the sea, but in no time was pushed back by the strong tidal current. Looking around the causeway he dragged several small logs together, lashing them with the strong weeds, near the water edge. By now the sky was turning a bright gold and he decided to try and reach the far shore before sunset. He pushed the small raft onto the oncoming waves thrashing his feet to overcome the strong current. After a long struggle, he was past the heavy waves and pushed on to the far side. On the shore in the distance he could see men and women, naked dancing a ritual around the huge fire. He now felt he had reached his journeys end and would now be at peace with himself and his fellow brothers and sisters, joining in with their ritual and customs. Suddenly, a small group of men broke away and grabbed a woman, dragging her towards the fire.

To his horror, they lifted her over their heads and hurled her onto the roaring flames where she convulsed, thrashed for a second before becoming engulfed in the flames. The acrid stench of burning flesh repulsed him and now understanding the reason for the sacrifice struck horror into his heart. Men and women were satiating their hunger, feeding on each other. Hanging his head, all his efforts now seemed futile and cried out in anger. The horror of it all shocked him into realising that he wished he never had these strange thoughts and emotions which made him wander and forced him to stray from the garden.

He paddled the raft furiously away from the shore heading out toward the sea. The strong current took hold of the flimsy raft pulling it further out into the foreboding sea. The sky darkened, the waves began to rise and fall, threatening the advent of an oncoming storm.

THROUGH THE MAELSTROM

The Mariner stared out on the calm sea. The gentle swell of the turning tide, gently rocked the small fishing boats back and forth on their moorings. The ink-black night sky, encrusted with bright diamond stars shone brightly with the waning moon. There was a kind breeze gently feathering the oily black sea, which was a respite from the long hot humid day that lay ahead.

He often came out in the early hours of the morning to spend time alone, to think of the day before him. Today had been especially good reason for getting away alone with his thoughts. He had left the village with the moon still high after having an argument with his father over his religious duties.

His father had complained of the Mariner leaving the oil lamp to run dry. He now thought about the argument. His father, strong willed, adhered strictly to his religious scripture, and was daily intent on imposing his will and religious beliefs onto his wife and sons. He loved his father and tried his best to emulate him in his religious duties, but it invariably left the Mariner feeling empty and alone. The many rituals his father practised only confirmed the Mariners conviction that his family's religious duties held no substance, were superficial and had no depth of meaning. He often pondered the existence of a god that could be personal to him, but the hypocrisy of the villagers and the secrets that went on with the men-folk, made him cynical and he would quickly dismiss it from his thoughts. If there was god, he certainly did not hold him in any great favour, he thought. His life and its tedious repetition of daily ritual convinced him that there was no great purpose to his existence, considering the meaningless life which he had been made to endure.

It had not been long since the visitors had arrived, but had already made a lasting impression on the Mariner. They had travelled from the mainland, which it was possible to see a faint outline of its shore on a clear day. The old men folk told stories of long ago that some islanders had sailed to the mainland and had travelled far into the country. They had finally reached a high plateau, which on climbing; they saw a large forest with a silver stream winding its way in the distance. It had been rumoured that beyond the forest they saw was a deep chasm with snow-capped mountains high above. The more superstitious of the old folk told of a traveller who had been washed ashore on a small raft from the mainland and who possessed strange healing powers.

His family, having lived for generations on the small group of islands, objected to his interest in the recent arrival of men and women from the mainland. Their ways were much different from the way the islanders viewed things. For one, they were more clever in the way they lit fires, using hard stones to spark the dry wood to flames. Their religious custom, of praying over the animals, before they were put to the knife. Their insistence that one prayed to only one god to attain enlightenment. Their rotunda places of worship contained no statues, or images with which to perform their religious rituals. These ways conflicted with the islander's customs and were considered blasphemous by many of the islanders. To the mariner they seemed rational and liberating. His feelings told him that these humble, pious men and women offered a better way towards fulfilling a spiritual life.

He reflected on the visit he had made to their place of worship. Unlike his own religion the priests were allowed to marry and raise a family. The absence of statues on the walls in their place of worship was replaced by long shelves where thousands of books of religious scripture, astronomy and science were placed, available to all worshippers for study and debate. The one who oversaw the running of their place of worship and prayer took the Mariner aside to a small vestibule. He explained that before prayer they must first observe a ritual of cleansing and rinsing of the mouth in order commence the purification process, which would be completed when, during prayer they would submit their will and seek guidance in all their deeds to Him who has all power. He then asked the Mariner many things about his own religion, which he commenced to describe.

The visitors face took on an alarmed look when the Mariner explained of an action of a predecessor in their history from a far distant past. He questioned him, asking, why should you carry the fear and guilt for the sin of another man

The Mariner eventually left their place of worship after eating, praying and studying the ways of these gentle people from the mainland. He now felt a new power in his heart which liberated him of any feelings of guilt and realised that the rituals and customs of his own people, actually enslaved, rather than liberated its followers. For the first time in his life he was forced by reason to realise that his own customs and religion were far inferior to the visitors from the mainland and now began to understand the controlling ways and insidious power of customs and ritual passed down through many generations of belief.

The golden sun crept slowly over the horizon, welcoming the coming day. Bright rays of light began to light the sky creating silhouettes of the fishing boats, and casting shadows on the sea. The sky was growing lighter and the Mariner could just make out the faint outline of his father's house and a lamplight from a small window. He thought of his father and brothers preparing themselves for their daily monotonous ritual, praying before images to enhance the purpose to their prayer.

Faintly, in the far distance he could hear a light voice calling the visitor's to prayer at their rotunda place of worship. The Mariner stood transfixed for a moment listening to the soft plaintive voice, feeling an emotional attachment to these pious gentle people.

He thought of his family and the different conflicting ways between them and himself. The dawning light allowed the Mariner to go through his routine of checking over the boat and his supply of water, placing the clay jug close to the tiller. He had lit two small lamps at the prow of the boat which cast a bright yellow light on the sea offering direction away from the dark grey rocks each side of the inlet. He tied the tiller fast and cast off, whilst setting the oars. He pulled at the oars with all his strength against the strong currents. The small boat rose gently to the light oncoming waves and slowly eased off its moorings. He shipped his oars and unfurled the light sail from the tall mast, making it fast. The light sail bellowed out catching the light breeze as the boat steered clear of the inlet. The mariner felt the strong tug of the currents on the tiller and steered towards the rising sun. The tide had risen and the Mariner's small fishing boat slowly eased out on to the sea.

The wind had strengthened, filling the sail, pulling the boat far away from the safety of the inlet. The Mariner peered back towards the shore and could see small lights blinking out on the houses of the village. The sun was slowly rising golden, the dark heavens, turning a pale blue and then dark blue across the horizon. The pale green sea, each side of the boat swirled against the prow casting white foam flecks on the waves. Small fish darted, translucent just below the surface, following the prow of the boat. The Mariner stared at the rising sun for a long time as the boat sailed further out to sea.

He was far away from shore and looking back could see the faint outline of his village in the far distance. He turned back and stared in awe at the vast expanse of sea before him, the sky above, the pale outline of the moon, the bright stars fading with the coming day. He pondered the existence of some mighty force behind it all and thought that maybe his parents could be right but then his mind snapped shut at the suggestion. How could any god want to be part of such deceit and hypocrisy. He thought of the visitors and felt that their goodness and piety could be enough to offer him the comfort and answer to his futile existence. But it still did not satisfy the deep longing for something real in his life, something he could communicate with or even talk to.

He sailed further out to sea until he could no longer see the islands. The wind suddenly dropped and folding the light sail, made it fast to the tall mast. He extinguished the two small lamps at the prow and stowed them at the helm of the boat. His mouth was dry and reached for the clay water jug, close to the tiller. The sky was much brighter and the sun was warm on his face. He settled down and lay for a while shading his eyes from the bright sunlight.

His mind drifted to the early morning at his father's house and the argument. He frowned and felt a great weariness in his mind and body and with the gentle lapping of the waves against the hull of the boat; closed his eyes.

He opened his eyes and was laying under a tree in a large meadow. He was on a grass verge near a river bank. There were small squat trees close near where a stream met and flowed over a waterfall, down in to the main river flow. In the distance was a thicket which led into a dark forest. A large yellow butterfly landed on the damp grass near his elbow. He stared for a while transfixed at its beauty and the butterfly appeared to stare back at him. It seemed to smile and shaking his head in disbelief, raised himself from the grass. The butterfly's wings seemed to vibrate giving off a sweet musical note; fluttered suspended for a moment and flew on to a fine branch of the tree he sat under.

He suddenly heard a voice call in the distance and turned to see a young man frantically running naked towards the entrance to the forest. He looked around and saw that he was in a Garden. He felt quite calm and familiar with the surrounding, feeling quite sure that he had been there before. He closed his eyes, breathing in the sweet scents of the meadow. He thought of his family and the visitors, but no longer felt the confusion and anguish he had felt before. Everything seemed exactly as it should be and felt the consciousness of a powerful presence all around him. He was home; he thought and would never leave the Garden.

'Dinhra,' a soft voice whispered. 'Dinhra.' The Mariner sat up abruptly, hearing his name. 'Dinhra', the voice whispered, 'you have just started your journey, you lost your innocence in another time, but you will have to travel much further to regain it.'

The large yellow butterfly alighted on his shoulder and whispered, 'Dinhra you must leave the Garden. Open your eyes.'

He opened his eyes and felt a fine rain wetting his face. He felt for the first time to be at peace with himself and the feeling of a powerful presence like a gentle blissful breeze was blowing around and through him.

He was brought back abruptly with a jolt when a large wave hit his frail craft sideways almost capsizing the small boat. He quickly, hoisted a small sail in order to stabilise it. The small boat lurched and swung with each swelling wave and he struggled desperately to control it and stop it capsizing.

He looked around hoping to see some sign of land, but whilst asleep, all around him, dark rain clouds had gathered and a strong wind was pulling the boat faster with the hoisted sail. He leaned back on the tiller with his bare feet pressed hard against the bottom of the boat. The waves grew stronger and the Mariner realised the strong winds and currents were pulling the small boat further out to sea. The sun suddenly switched off like a light, a large black rain cloud casting dark shadows on the sea. The frail craft raised itself up on a crest of a huge wave and another followed crashing down on the frail craft, throwing the Mariner into the dark foreboding sea.

He clutched desperately at a piece of broken mast and raised himself up with one arm to keep his head above water. He gasped for air as another wave raised him still higher above the sea and cast him down into the dark waters, letting go his grasp on the broken mast. The sun pierced the broken rain clouds, momentarily casting light as a torrential downpour fanned the sunlit sea. He struggled to remove his clothing and finally wriggled free, enabling him to swim freely. He could see in the distance the helm and the tiller still intact. He cried out and with great effort swam towards the floating timber and managed to straddle himself across the splintered helm and clutched the tiller with both arms. The waves grew higher and the Mariner clung desperately to the tiller which turned with each crashing wave dragging him under the water with each roll.

The sky darkened and the wind suddenly dropped leaving an uncanny calmness to the water surrounding him. As far as the Mariner could see, a great circle of water appeared and slowly started to turn creating a vortex and started dragging the Mariner with it.

'The Maelstrom! He cried. He had often heard stories told of it appearing from nowhere and trapping large fishing vessels in its wake, dragging them down to the depths of the sea, only to find the wreckage the other side of the islands a long time after. He cried out, 'Oh God help me! I do not want to die! I should never have doubted you! I just do not know how to believe in you. I want to believe but I am so confused.'

He hoisted himself over the tiller sobbing and crying in despair. He knew all was lost. He strained to see any land insight, but all around was the vast expanse of sea surrounding him. He then realised the significance of the feeling he had when he first heard the visitors call to prayer and when he marvelled in awe at the great expanse of sea when first setting sail.

What he confused with spirituality were merely emotions, which were fleeting and soon gone. He now realised that, God is not something external, having to perform ritual in order to gain access to His favours, something to be prayed to, but rather He was present from within and always had and will exist, so long as one believed and had faith in Him.

He no longer felt afraid and believed, took one last look around the great expanse of sea and released his grip on the tiller, pushing it away from him. The maelstrom gripped his frail naked body drawing it ever closer to the centre of the vortex, dragging him down into the dark waters.'

RETURN TO THE GARDEN

A dark red turgid sun slowly rose, half covering the horizon. Long orange flames of fire shot out into the dark purple sky. A large pale moon hung pink and iridescent, slowly rising tandem in permanent twilight. The oily black sea slowly heaved and swelled, carrying white flecks of foam, seeping across encrusted ridges of salt at the water's edge.

The man lay prone on the black sand, his body just above the water's edge. A fine mist hung over the sea from which he had stumbled. Lying on his side, he slowly raised his head and looked up the high hill and then back along the long sandy causeway. He lay for a while and tried to recall the events leading up to the time he had stumbled out of the sea. His arrival and the journey he had traversed was but a faint memory.

He rolled onto his back and twisted his space helmet, giving off a faint hiss and raising his hands, tossed it away from him. He wearily sat up and could see his small spacecraft slowly swaying to and fro on the black oily sea. The cockpit door was swinging ajar allowing the viscous sea to pour into the spacecraft. It was slowly submerging while large oily bubbles rose to the surface around the gaping hole of the cockpit. He struggled to stand and shrugged his space suit down to his waist, pushing it down to his ankles and stepped outside of it.

The heat was stifling and the acrid smell of lichen, near the water's edge gave off a bright green fluoresent glow. A fine mist was rising and he could see the faint outline of a group of islands in the far distance. He had viewed the islands as his spacecraft sped over the mainland and was looking for a place to ditch the small spacecraft, which had lost its main-power drives as the result of an electric storm. He finally brought the spacecraft parallel to the group of islands and the mainland before plunging into the black oily sea.

The dark purple sky momentarily gave off blinding lightning strikes over the horizon, the sulphurous vapours adding to the fetid heat. The small spacecraft gave a final gasp of air and disappeared below the sea. He looked around the causeway and sensed he had stood at the same spot in a time long past.

Rhadin a voice seemed to say in his head, you are hallucinating from the long time travel. You have never walked on this world until now and memory dictates that you complete your task as others have done before you. This world will soon reach its end, but other worlds will follow and take its place, just as it has always been and always will be.

He turned and looked up the high hill and started to climb, the black sand hot sand beneath his feet.

Rhadin stood at the top of the hill and looked down across the causeway to the group of islands in the distance. A strong hot wind blew in from the sea and heavy rain began to fall soaking his long black hair.

He looked up at the huge dying sun, the moon slowly creating a partial eclipse. The time had come, Rhadin thought. He turned towards the mainland and could just define a small wood thick with young trees and bushes. It all seemed so familiar and the feeling returned that he had been here before but, immediately, put it out of his mind. This is absurd, he thought to himself. I have travelled 100 million light spans from my mother planet. Have traversed several galaxies to this desolate globe; it is madness to think I have visited this planet before. Never the less, he felt a presentiment of some future event which would decide his ultimate destiny. He suddenly felt weary and the oppressive heat weighed heavily on his body. He fought against the idea of resting and felt a will not of his own forcing him to stumble forward towards the small wood with the hope of receiving some shelter in the bushes in the far distance.

With each step his breathing became more laboured and finally reaching the wood, leaned against a small tree, panting heavily. He tried to stand erect, in order to get his bearings and stumbled to his knees, before rolling on his back.

He must have passed out for a while, because when he came around the sun had disappeared and the moon was slowly sinking below the horizon and giving a faint glow to the small trees and bushes where he lay. Everywhere else was blackness.

He felt a great weariness in his mind and body and squinting noticed a blur image hovering to the right of his shoulder. He turned and a large yellow butterfly slowly, came into focus. He stared transfixed for what seemed and age and closing his eyes he realised that he was reliving events of a time long past.

He slowly opened his eyes and the yellow butterfly fluttered towards him and hovered just above Rahdin's face and whispered gently, 'come, Rhadin, let us leave this wilderness and return to whence we came.' Rhadin stood up and obediently followed the butterfly through the small wood away from the causeway and sea. He followed the large yellow butterfly through the dense woodland, staying close.

Rhadin trudged on for an age, keeping in sight of the butterfly, which gave off a shimmering bright gold light with which Rhadin could follow in the blackness.

Eventually, the yellow butterfly turned and fluttered towards Rhadin and alighted on his shoulder, whispered gently in his ear, 'we shall rest here for a while'. Rhadin sat hunched on a large black rock, resting his back against a small tree. The yellow butterfly alighted a small bush near his right shoulder and whispering asked, 'Rhadin, do you know why you are here and what tasks you have to perform?

Rhadin gave a puzzled look and slowly shook his head. 'Well then,' asked the butterfly, 'do you remember anything about your journey to this dying planet and who has come before you? Rhadin raised his, head, thought hard for a moment and said, 'I seemed to remember as a child being told that I possessed special powers that would be beneficent to the future of our planet, I recall being treated differently from my brothers and sisters and much to my distress, being taken from my parents, whom I loved very much.'

'What happened then? enquired the butterfly. Rhadin started to tremble and cried, 'they separated me from my mother and father and family and told me they were preparing me for a long journey'. Do you know why? Enquired the butterfly. Rhadin, shook his head.

'Well, soon there will come a time and place when everything will be revealed to you, but, come we still have a long way to go,' said the butterfly. Rhadin stood up and obediently followed the butterfly through the blackness, until they were suddenly out of the wood. They continued on their sojourn and in time the sky grew lighter and took on a pale blue countenance. The air had also became cooler and a gentle breeze was blowing in from the west.

Rhadin's step was easier and the previous tiredness he felt when leaving the causeway had left him. Looking up, Rhadin saw in the far distance a dried out river bed and hastened his step until he reached the pebbled bed of the dried out stream. He turned and noticed in his haste to reach the riverbed the butterfly had disappeared from view.

Rhadin sat on the edge of the pebbled riverbed and laying back, closing his eyes he drifted off into a twilight sleep. Still aware of his surroundings a picture appeared in his mind's eye of a naked man running out of a garden into a dense forest. The picture faded and another appeared of the same man setting sail on a small raft out into the sea from the causeway where he had arrived in his spacecraft. The picture faded and clouds swirled and another picture appeared of a man sat near his small sailing craft preparing it for a trip out to sea. He finally cast off and travelled far out of the harbour into the deep ocean. The flimsy craft could be seen being drawn towards a great vortex.

The picture faded and another appeared of Rhadin being prepared for his long journey in hypersleep. Rhadin suddenly opened his eyes startled saw the shimmering gold presence of the yellow butterfly.

'Well, Rhadin, are you still puzzled to your purpose and journey to this desolate planet? Rhadin slowly shook his head and replied, 'Never more puzzled than I am now,' he replied.

The yellow butterfly alighted on his bare shoulder and whispered, 'In time all will be revealed, but for the present we need to travel further west and discover your true purpose.'

Rhadin, stood up and obediently followed the yellow butterfly down through the deep dry pebbled river bed, up to the other side and onto a vast plain.

They travelled for a further sunset until they finally arrived at a plateau. He stood on the edge of the plateau looking down on a large desolate plain and beyond a forest. Beyond the forest below him was a silver stream winding its way and bending out of sight of the plain and in the far distance, there was a garden.

They traversed down the long hillock until they reached the edge of the forest and without hesitation entered into the dimly lit surroundings. Rhadin looked up and could see the bright sunlight piercing the tall trees and bushes and a pale blue sky, with wisps of clouds, passing slowly overhead.

A small stream flowed down through a ridge and the yellow butterfly followed the stream, in the direction of the garden. Rhadin followed and breathed in the sweet pungent smell of the pine forest. His step lightened and spontaneously started into a run, passing the yellow butterfly. He seemed to run effortlessly and his legs grew strong with every step. He eventually slowed down and stopped, stooping, drank thirstily from the stream.

The yellow butterfly appeared from above and alighting on his bare shoulder, whispered, sweetly, 'almost journeys end Rhadin.' They continued to travel further west as the sun grew warmer and eventually came to an opening in the forest.

Rhadin gasped and gazed in awe at the view of a beautiful garden and in the far distance a group of squat trees. The yellow butterfly flew without hesitation into the heart of the garden, Rhadin following quickly.

They arrived at the group of squat trees where the river met the stream and the yellow butterfly beckoned Rhadin in the shade of a tree.

The grass felt damp and warm and Rhadin sat with his knees raised and his hands behind his head. The yellowy butterfly hovered above Rhadin's head and asked, 'do you recall the dream you had at the pebbled stream? 'Yes, I do,' answered Rhadin and added, 'but it was not so much a dream, but in the form of a message, at least that is how it seemed to me,'

The yellow butterfly gave of a sweet shrill sound and said, 'Rhadin you are now at the end of the final message, as you call it and are sat exactly where Hindra sat in that time long past and went on to say, 'you see Hindra desired nothing and was quite content to live in the Garden with his family, until the Garden gave him the chance to question his loyalty and lose his innocence.' Rhadin, looked puzzled and asked, 'But why should he wish to do that? and added 'I always thought that innocence was something to be cherished and valued.' 'Yes, maybe,' answered the yellow butterfly, 'but Hindra's innocence was not true innocence in the real sense, because it had not been earned, but was given as a free gift from the Garden and Hindra had to lose his innocence to regain it and to realise its true worth,' added the yellow butterfly.'
'But Hindra was left alone and afraid at the end of the message and wished to return to the Garden,' exclaimed Rhadin. 'Yes, but you must realise that Hindra's search for something new and exciting with his new feelings, now he had left the Garden had left him with nothing more that self and his new found knowledge.'

'In the case of the second message,' the yellow butterfly continued, 'Dhinra, the Mariner was full of doubt about his existence and his families obsession with their religion. Now his encounter with the new arrivals at his islands seemed to offer him an answer to his life and the problems he felt he had, but he was in fact, searching for the unattainable and was asking something for nothing and realised this and made his final surrender, just before his demise in the maelstrom.'

'But what of me then? asked Rhadin. 'What is my purpose and why all the mystery surrounding my voyage to this far distant planet? 'This far distance planet? The yellow butterfly asked, 'are you still not sure of your purpose in the first two messages and your reason for being here? Rhadin, thought for a while and slowly shook his head. 'No, it is still a complete mystery to me and will need explaining,' replied Rhadin.

'But don't you see,' said the yellow butterfly, 'there is nothing to explain. The fact that you gave up your life and devoted yourself to this journey without question, is enough in itself. The fact that you wish to carry out this third message, without reward, is the answer and this makes the previous messages complete, in that you only desire to serve, expecting nothing in return.'

'Then, who are you? enquired Rhadin 'and what is your purpose in all this? 'That is quite simple,' the butterfly answered. 'I am the Garden and I am also Hindra, Dhinra and will soon be you, now close your eyes and rest, it has been a long and tiring journey for both you and I.' Rhadin slowly smiled at the yellow butterfly and nodding his head, laid back on the warm grass and closing his eyes, fell gently to sleep.

Rhadin awoke suddenly and felt different; he turned and could see the yellow butterfly on the damp grass next to him. 'But I don't understand,' said Rhadin.

'You have metamorphosed into a yellow butterfly and completed the cycle,' replied the yellow butterfly and our journey is at an end, but paradoxically, is just beginning. You see Rhadin, our perception of the world is only what we see and understand of it and our individual selves, which is our immediate surroundings. There is a much larger view when seen from the Garden's perspective.' The yellow butterfly alighted on to a small thorny bush. 'Come Rhadin, let us see the Garden in its true light.' Rhadin flew on to a branch close to the butterfly and without hesitation the yellow butterfly flew high into the air, Rhadin following.'

They both flew higher and higher until they could see the whole of the Garden and the surrounding forest and snow capped mountain. Still higher they flew and the causeway came into view and then the Mariner's village. They flew through the wispy clouds and below a large modern city appeared with tall skyscrapers and a mass of motorways converging on each other, they flew still higher...'

Made in the USA
Columbia, SC
09 July 2018